The Delectable D

The Delectable Duchy

by Arthur Quiller-Couch

PROLOGUE.

A week ago, my friend the Journalist wrote to remind me that once upon a time I had offered him a bed in my cottage at Troy and promised to show him the beauties of the place. He was about (he said) to give himself a fortnight's holiday, and had some notion of using that time to learn what Cornwall was like. He could spare but one day for Troy, and hardly looked to exhaust its attractions; nevertheless, if my promise held good.... By anticipation he spoke of my home as a "nook." Its windows look down upon a harbour, wherein, day by day, vessels of every nation and men of large experience are for ever going and coming; and beyond the harbour, upon leagues of open sea, highway of the vastest traffic in the world: whereas from his own far more expensive house my friend sees only a dirty laurel-bush, a high green fence, and the upper half of a suburban lamp post. Yet he is convinced that I dwell in a nook.

I answered his letter, warmly repeating the invitation; and last week he arrived. The change had bronzed his face, and from his talk I learnt that he had already seen half the Duchy, in seven days. Yet he had been unreasonably delayed in at least a dozen places, and used the strongest language about 'bus and coach communication, local trains, misleading sign-posts, and the like. Our scenery enraptured him—every aspect of it. He had travelled up the Tamar to Launceston, crossed the moors, climbing Roughtor and Brown Willy on his way, plunged down towards Camelford, which he appeared to have reached by following two valleys simultaneously, coached to Boscastle, walked to Tintagel, climbed up to Uther's Castle, diverged inland to St. Nectan's Kieve, driven on to Bedruthan Steps, Mawgan, the Vale of Lanherne, Newquay, taken a train thence to Truro, a steamer from Truro to Falmouth, crossed the ferry to St. Mawes, walked up the coast to Mevagissey, driven from Mevagissey to St. Austell, and at St. Austell taken another train for Troy. This brought half his holiday to a close: the remaining half he meant to devote to the Mining District, St. Ives, the Land's End, St. Michael's Mount, the Lizard, and perhaps the Scilly Isles.

Then I began to feel that I lived in a nook, and to wonder how I could spin out its attractions to cover a whole day: for I could not bear to think of his departing with secret regret for his lavished time. In a flash I saw the truth; that my love for this spot is built up of numberless trivialities, of small memories all incommunicable, or ridiculous when communicated; a scrap of local speech heard at this corner, a pleasant native face remembered in that doorway, a battered vessel dropping anchor—she went out in the spring with her crew singing dolefully; and the grey-bearded man waiting in his boat beneath her counter till the custom-house officers have made their survey is the father of one among the crew, and is waiting to take his son's hand again, after months of absence. Would this interest my friend, if I pointed it out to him? Or, if I walk with him by the path above the creek, what will he care to know that on this particular bank the violets always bloom earliest—that one of a line of yews that top the churchyard wall is remarkable because a pair of missel-thrushes have chosen it to build in for three successive years? The violets are gone. The empty nest has almost dissolved under the late heavy rains, and the yew is so like its fellows that I myself have no idea why the birds chose it. The longer I reflected the more certain I felt that my friend could find all he wanted in the guide-books.

None the less, I did my best: rowed him for a mile or two up the river; took him out to sea, and along the coast for half a dozen miles. The water was choppy, as it is under the slightest breeze from the south-east; and the Journalist was sea-sick; but seemed to mind this very little, and recovered sufficiently to ask my boatman two or three hundred questions before we reached the harbour again. Then we landed and explored the Church. This took us some time, owing to several freaks in its construction, for which I blessed the memory of its early-English builders. We went on to the Town Hall, the old Stannary Prison (now in ruins), the dilapidated Block-houses, the Battery. We traversed the town from end to end and studied the barge-boards and punkin-ends of every old house. I had meanly ordered that dinner should be ready half-an-hour earlier than usual, and, as it was, the objects of interest just lasted out.

As we sat and smoked our cigarettes after dinner, the Journalist said—

"If you don't mind, I'll be off in a few minutes and shut myself up in your study. I won't be long turning out the copy; and after that I can talk to you without feeling I've neglected my work. There's an early post here, I suppose?"

"Man alive!" said I, "you don't mean to tell me that you're working, this holiday?"

"Only a letter for the 'Daily ——' three times a week—a column and a half, or so."

"The subject?"

"Oh, descriptive stuff about the places I've been visiting. I call it 'An Idler in Lyonesse.'"

"Why Lyonesse?"

"Why not?"

"Well, Lyonesse has lain at the bottom of the Atlantic, between Land's End and Scilly, these eight hundred years. The chroniclers relate that it was overwhelmed and lost in 1099, A.D. If your Constant Readers care to ramble there, they're welcome, I'm sure."

"I had thought" said he, "it was just a poet's name for Cornwall. Well, never mind, I'll go in presently and write up this place: it's just as well to do it while one's impressions are still fresh."

4

He finished his coffee, lit a fresh cigarette, and strolled off to the little library where I usually work. I stepped out upon the verandah and looked down on the harbour at my feet, where already the vessels were hanging out their lamps in the twilight. I had looked down thus, and at this hour, a thousand times; and always the scene had something new to reveal to me, and much more to withhold—small subtleties such as a man finds in his wife, however ordinary she may appear to other people. And here, in the next room, was a man who, in half-a-dozen hours, felt able to describe Troy, to deck her out, at least, in language that should captivate a million or so of breakfasting Britons.

"My country," said I, "if you have given up, in these six hours, a tithe of your heart to this man—if, in fact, his screed be not arrant bosh—then will I hie me to London for good and all, and write political leaders all the days of my life."

In an hour's time the Journalist came sauntering out to me, and announced that his letter was written.

"Have you sealed it up?"

"Well, no. I thought you might give me an additional hint or two; and maybe I might look it over again and add a few lines before turning in."

"Do you mind my seeing it?"

"Not the least in the world, if you care to. I didn't think, though, that it could possibly interest you, who know already every mortal thing that is to be known about the place."

"You're mistaken. I may know all about this place when I die, but not before. Let's hear what you have to say."

We went indoors, and he read it over to me.

It was a surprisingly brilliant piece of description; and accurate, too. He had not called it "a little fishing-town," for instance, as so many visitors have done in my hearing, though hardly a fishing-boat puts out from the harbour. The guide-books call it a fishing-town, but the Journalist was not misled, though he had gone to them for a number of facts. I corrected a date and then sat silent. It amazed me that a man who could see so much, should fail to perceive that what he had seen was of no account in comparison with what he had not: or that, if he did indeed perceive this, he could write such stuff with such gusto. "To be capable of so much and content with so little," I thought; and then broke off to wonder if, after all, he were not right. To-morrow he would be on his way, crowding his mind with quick and brilliant impressions, hurrying, living, telling his fellows a thousand useful and pleasant things, while I pored about to discover one or two for them.

"I thought," said the Journalist, swinging his gold pencil-case between finger and thumb, "you might furnish me with just a hint or so, to give the thing a local colour. Some little characteristic of the natives, for instance. I noticed, this afternoon, when I was most sea-sick, that your fellow took off his hat and pulled something out of the lining. I was too ill to see what it was; but he dropped it overboard the next minute and muttered something."

"Oh, you remarked that, did you?"

"Yes, and meant to ask him about it afterwards; but forgot, somehow."

"Do you remember where we were—what we were passing—when he did this?"

"Not clearly. I was infernally ill just then. Why did he do it?"

I was silent.

"I suppose it had some meaning?" he went on.

"Yes, it had. And excuse me when I say that I'm hanged if either you or your Constant Readers shall know what that meaning was. My dear fellow, you belong to a strong race—a race that has beaten us and taken toll of us, and now carves 'Smith' and 'Thompson' and such names upon our fathers' tombs. But there are some things you have not laid hands on yet; secrets that we all know somehow, but never utter, even among ourselves, nor allude to. If I told you what Billy Tredegar did to-day, and why he did it, I tell you frankly your article would make some thousands of Constant Readers open wide eyes over their breakfast-cups. But you won't know. Why, after all, should I say anything to spoil Cornwall's prospects as a health-resort?"

My friend took this very quietly, merely observing that it was rather late in the day to take sides against Hengist and Horsa. But he was sorry, I could see, to lose his local colour. And as I looked down, for the last time that night, upon Troy, this petition escaped me—

"O my country, if I keep your secrets, keep for me your heart!"

THE SPINSTER'S MAYING.

"The fields breathe sweet, the daisies kiss our feet,
Young lovers meet, old wives a-sunning sit;
In every street these tunes our ears do greet—
* Cuckoo, jug-jug, pu-wee, to-witta-woo!*
*   Spring, the sweet Spring."*

At two o'clock on May morning a fishing-boat, with a small row-boat in tow, stole up the harbour between the lights of the vessels that lay at anchor. She came on a soundless tide, with her sprit-mainsail wide and drawing, and her foresail flapping idle; and although her cuddy-top and gunwale glistened wet with a recent shower, the man who steered her looked over his shoulder at the waning moon, and decided that the dawn would be a fine one. A furlong below the Town Quay he left the tiller and lowered sail: two furlongs above, he dropped anchor: then, having made all ship-shape, he lit a pipe and pulled an enormous watch from his fob. The vessels he had passed since entering the harbour's mouth seemed one and all asleep. But a din of horns, kettles, and tea-trays, and a wild tattoo of door-knockers, sounded along the streets behind the stores and houses that lined the water-side. Already the town-boys were ushering in the month of May.

The man waited until the half-hour chimed over the 'long-shore roofs from the church-tower up the hill; set his watch with care; and sat down to wait for the sun. Upon the wooded cliff that faces the town the birds were waking; and by-and-bye, from the three small quays came the sound of voices laughing, and then a boat or two stealing out of the shadow, each crowded with boys and

6

maids. Before the dawn grew red above the cliff where the birds sang, a dozen boats had gone by him on their way up the river, the chatter and broken laughter returning down its dim reaches long after the rowers had passed out of sight.

For some moments longer he watched the broadening daylight, till the sun, mounting above the cliff, blazed on the watch he had again pulled out and now shut with a brisk snap. His round, shaven face, still boyish in middle age, wore the shadow of a solemn responsibility. He clambered out into the small boat astern, and, casting loose, pulled towards a bright patch of colour in the grey shore wall: a blue quay-door overhung with ivy. The upper windows of the cottage behind it were draped with snowy muslin, and its walls, coated with recent whitewash, shamed its neighbours to right and left.

As the boat dropped under this blue quay-door, its upper flap opened softly, and a voice as softly said—

"Thank you kindly, John. And how d'ye do this May morning?"

"Charming," the man answered frankly. "Handsome weather 'tis, to be sure."

He looked up and smiled at her, like a lover.

"I needn't to ask how *you* be; for you'm looking sweet as blossom," he went on.

And yet the woman that smiled down on him was fifty years old at least. Her hair, which usually lay in two flat bands, closely drawn over the temples, had for this occasion been worked into waves by curling-papers, and twisted in front of either ear, into that particular ringlet locally called a kiss-me-quick. But it was streaked with grey, and the pinched features wore the tint of pale ivory.

"D'ye think you can clamber down the ladder, Sarah? The tide's fairly high."

"I'm afraid I'll be showing my ankles."

"I was hoping so. Wunnerful ankles you've a-got, Sarah, and a wunnerful cage o' teeth. Such extremities 'd well beseem a king's daughter, all glorious within!"

Sarah Blewitt pulled open the lower flap of the door and set her foot on the ladder. She wore a white print gown beneath her cloak, and a small bonnet of black straw decorated with sham cowslips. The cloak, hitching for a moment on the ladder's side, revealed a beaded reticule that hung from her waist, and clinked as she descended.

"I reckon there's scarce an inch of paint left on my front door," she observed, as the man steadied her with an arm round her waist, and settled her comfortably in the stern-sheets.

He unshipped his oars and began to pull.

"Ay. I heard 'em whackin' the door with a deal o' tow-row. They was going it like billy-O when I came past the Town Quay. But one mustn' complain, May-mornin's."

"I wasn' complaining," said the woman; "I was just remarking. How's Maria?"

"She's nicely, thank you."

"And the children?"

7

"Brave."

"I've put up sixpennyworth of nicey in four packets—that's one apiece—and I've written the name on each, for you to take home to 'em."

She fumbled in her reticule and produced the packets. The peppermint-drops and brandy-balls were wrapped in clean white paper, and the names written in a thin Italian hand. John thanked her and stowed them in his trousers pockets.

"You'll give my love to Maria? I take it very kindly her letting you come for me like this."

"Oh, as for that—" began John, and broke off; "I don't call to mind that ever I saw a more handsome morning for the time o' year."

They had made this expedition together more than a score of times, and always found the same difficulty in conversing. The boat moved easily past the town, the jetties above it, and the vessels that lay off them awaiting their cargoes; it turned the corner and glided by woods where the larches were green, the sycamores dusted with bronze, the wild cherry-trees white with blossom, and all voluble. Every little bird seemed ready to burst his throat that morning with the deal he had to say. But these two—the man especially—had nothing to say, yet ached for words.

"Nance Treweek's married," the woman managed to tell him at last.

"I was thinking it likely, by the way she carried on last Maying."

"That wasn' the man. She've kept company with two since him, and mated with a fourth man altogether—quite a different sort, in the commercial traveller line."

"Did he wear a seal weskit?"

"Well, he might have; but not to my knowledge. What makes you ask?"

"Because I used to know a Johnny Fortnight that wore one in these parts; and I thought it might be he, belike."

"Jim had a greater gift o' speech than you can make pretence to," said the woman abruptly. "I often wonder that of two twin-brothers one should be so glib and t'other so mum-chance."

"'Tis the Lord's ways," the man answered, resting on his oars. "Will you be dabblin' your feet as usual, Sarah?"

"Why not?"

He turned the boat's nose to a small landing-place cut in the solid rock, where a straight pathway dived between hazel-bushes and appeared again twenty feet above, winding inland around the knap of a green hill. Here he helped her to disembark, and waited with his back to the shore. The spinster behind the hazel screen pulled off shoes and stockings, and paddled about for a minute in the dewy grass that fringed the meadow's lower slope. Then, drawing a saucer from her reticule, she wrung some dew into it and bathed her face. Ten minutes later she re-appeared on the river's bank.

"A happy May, John!"

"A happy May to *you*, Sarah!"

John stepped out beside her, and making his boat fast, followed her up the narrow path and around the shoulder of the steep meadow. They overed a stile, then a second, and were among pink slopes of orchards in bloom. Ahead of them a church tower rose out of soft billows of apple-blossom, and above the tower a lark was singing. A child came along the footpath from the village with two garlands mounted cross-wise on a pole and looped together with strings of painted birds' eggs. John gave him a penny for his show.

"Here's luck to your lass!" said the wise child.

Sarah was pleased, and added a second penny from her reticule. The boy spat on it for luck, slipped it into his breeches pocket, and went on his way skipping.

They stood still and looked after him for some moments, out of pure pleasure in his good humour; then descended among the orchards to the village. Half-way up the street stood the inn, the Flowing Source, with whitewashed front and fuchsia-trees that reached to the first-floor windows; and before it a well enclosed with a round stone wall, over which the toadflax spread in a tangle. Around the well, in the sunshine, were set a dozen or more small tables, covered with white cloths, and two score at least of young people eating bread and cream and laughing. The landlady, a broad woman in a blue print gown, and large apron, came forward.

"Why, Miss Sarah, I'd nigh 'pon given you up. Your table's been spread this hour, an' at last I was forced to ask some o' the young folks if you was dead or no."

"Why should I be dead more than another?"

"Well, well—in the midst o' life, we're told. 'Tisn' only the ripe apples that the wind scatters. He that comes by your side to-day is but twin-brother to him that came wi' you the first time I mind 'ee, seemin' but yesterday. Eh, Miss Sarah, but I envied 'ee then, sittin' wi' hand in hand, an' but one bite taken out o' your bread an' cream; but I was just husband-high myself i' those days, an' couldn't make the men believe it."

"Mary Ann Jacobs," Miss Sarah broke out, "if 'twas not for the quality of your cream, I'd go a-mayin' elsewhere, for I can truly say I hate your way of talkin' from the bottom of my soul."

"Sarah," said John, wiping his mouth as he finished his bread and cream, "I'm a glum man, as you well know; an' why Providence drowned poor Jim, when it might have taken his twin image that hadn' half his mouth—speech, is past findin' out. But 'tis generally allowed that the grip o' my hand is uncommon like what Jim's used to be; an' when I gets home to-night, the first thing my old woman'll be sure to ask is 'Did 'ee give Sarah poor Jim's hand-clasp?'—an' what to say I shan't know, unless you honours me so far."

"'Tis uncommon good of Maria," said the woman simply, and stole her thin hand into his horny palm. She had done so, in answer to the same speech, more than twenty times.

"Not at all," said John.

His fingers closed over hers, and rested so. All but a few of the mayers had risen from the table, and were romping and chasing each other back to the boats, for the majority were shop-girls and apprentices, and must be back in time for business. But Miss Sarah was in no hurry.

"Not yet," she entreated, as John's grasp began to relax. He tightened it again and waited, while she leant back, breathing short, with half-closed eyes.

At length she said he might release her.

"I'm sure 'tis uncommon kind of Maria," she repeated.

"I don't see where the kindness comes in. Maria can have as good any day o' the year, an' don't appear to value it to that extent."

They walked back through the orchards in silence. At Miss Sarah's quay-door they parted, and John hoisted sail for his home around the corner of the coast.

DAPHNIS.

Has olim exuvias mihi perfidus ille reliquit,
Pignora cara sui: quae nunc ego limine in ipso,
Terra, tibi mando; debent haec pignora Daphnin—
Ducite ab urbe domum, mea, carmina, ducite Daphnin.

I knew the superstition lingered along the country-side: and I was sworn to find it. But the labourers and their wives smoothed all intelligence out of their faces as soon as I began to hint at it. Such is the way of them. They were my good friends, but had no mind to help me in this. Nobody who has not lived long with them can divine the number of small incommunicable mysteries and racial secrets chambered in their inner hearts and guarded by their hospitable faces. These alone the Celt withholds from the Saxon, and when he dies they are buried with him.

A chance word or two of my old nurse, by chance caught in some cranny of a child's memory and recovered after many days, told me that the charm was still practised by the woman-folk, or had been practised not long before her death. So I began to hunt for it, and, almost as soon, to believe the search hopeless. The new generation of girls, with their smart frocks, in fashion not more than six months behind London, their Board School notions, and their consuming ambition to "look like a lady"—were these likely to cherish a local custom as rude and primitive as the long-stone circles on the tors above? But they were Cornish; and of that race it is unwise to judge rashly. For years I had never a clue: and then, by Sheba Farm, in a forsaken angle of the coast, surprised the secret.

Sheba Farm stands high above Ruan sands, over which its windows flame at sunset. And I sat in the farm kitchen drinking cider and eating potato-cake, while the farmer's wife, Mrs. Bolverson, obligingly attended to my coat, which had just been soaked by a thunder-shower. It was August, and already the sun beat out again, fierce and strong. The bright drops that gemmed the tamarisk-bushes above the wall of the town-place were already fading under its heat; and I heard the voices of the harvesters up the lane, as they returned to the oat-field whence the storm had routed them. A bright parallelogram stretched from the window across the white kitchen-table, and reached the dim hollow of the open fire-place. Mrs. Bolverson drew the towel-horse, on which my coat was stretched, between it and the wood fire, which (as she held) the sunshine would put out.

"It's uncommonly kind of you, Mrs. Bolverson," said I, as she turned one sleeve of the coat towards the heat. "To be sure, if the women in these parts would speak out, some of them have done more than that for the men with an old coat."

She dropped the sleeve, faced round, and eyed me.

"What do you know of that?" she asked slowly, and as if her chest tightened over the words. She was a woman of fifty and more, of fine figure but a worn face. Her chief surviving beauty was a pile of light golden hair, still lustrous as a girl's. But her blue eyes—though now they narrowed on me suspiciously—must have looked out magnificently in their day.

"I fancy," said I, meeting them frankly enough, "that what you know and I don't on that matter would make a good deal."

She laughed harshly, almost savagely.

"You'd better ask Sarah Gedye, across the coombe. She buried a man's clothes one time, and—it might be worth your while to ask her what came o't."

If you can imagine a glint of moonlight running up the blade of a rapier, you may know the chill flame of spite and despite that flickered in her eyes then as she spoke.

"I take my oath," I muttered to myself, "I'll act on the invitation."

The woman stood straight upright, with her hands clasped behind her, before the deal table. She gazed, under lowered brows, straight out of window; and following that gaze, I saw across the coombe a mean mud hut, with a wall around it, that looked on Sheba Farm with the obtrusive humility of a poor relation.

"Does she—does Sarah Gedye—live down yonder?"

"What is that to you?" she enquired fiercely, and then was silent for a moment, and added, with another short laugh—

"I reckon I'd like the question put to her: but I doubt you've got the pluck."

"You shall see," said I; and taking my coat off the towel-horse, I slipped it on.

She did not turn, did not even move her head, when I thanked her for the shelter and walked out of the house.

I could feel those steel-blue eyes working like gimlets into my back as I strode down the hill and passed the wooden plank that lay across the stream at its foot. A climb of less than a minute brought me to the green gate in the wall of Sarah Gedye's garden patch; and here I took a look backwards and upwards at Sheba. The sun lay warm on its white walls, and the whole building shone against the burnt hillside. It was too far away for me to spy Mrs. Bolverson's blue print gown within the kitchen window, but I knew that she stood there yet.

The sound of a footstep made me turn. A woman was coming round the corner of the cottage, with a bundle of mint in her hand.

She looked at me, shook off a bee that had blundered against her apron, and looked at me again—a brown woman, lean and strongly made, with jet-black eyes set deep and glistening in an ugly face.

"You want to know your way?" she asked.

"No. I came to see you, if your name is Sarah Gedye."

"Sarah Ann Gedye is my name. What 'st want?"

I took a sudden resolution to tell the exact truth.

"Mrs. Gedye, the fact is I am curious about an old charm that was practised in these parts, as I know, till recently. The charm is this—When a woman guesses her lover to be faithless to her, she buries a suit of his old clothes to fetch him back to her. Mrs. Bolverson, up at Sheba yonder—"

The old woman had opened her mouth (as I know now) to curse me. But as Mrs. Bolverson's name escaped me, she turned her back, and walked straight to her door and into the kitchen. Her manner told me that I was expected to follow.

But I was not prepared for the face she turned on me in the shadow of the kitchen. It was grey as wood-ash, and the black eyes shrank into it like hot specks of fire.

"She—*she* set you on to ask me that?" She caught me by the coat and hissed out: "Come back from the door—don't let her see." Then she lifted up her fist, with the mint tightly clutched in it, and shook it at the warm patch of Sheba buildings across the valley.

"May God burn her bones, as He has smitten her body barren!"

"What do you know of this?" she cried, turning upon me again.

"I know nothing. That I have offered you some insult is clear: but—"

"Nay, you don't know—you don't know. No man would be such a hound. You don't know; but, by the Lord, you shall hear, here where you'm standin', an' shall jedge betwix' me an' that pale 'ooman up yonder. Stand there an' list to me.

"He was my lover more'n five-an'-thirty years agone. Who? That 'ooman's wedded man, Seth Bolverson. We warn't married"—this with a short laugh. "Wife or less than wife, he found me to his mind. She—she that egged you on to come an' flout me—was a pale-haired girl o' seventeen or so i' those times—a church-goin' mincin' strip of a girl—the sort you men-folk bow the knee to for saints. Her father owned Sheba Farm, an' she look'd across on my man, an' had envy on 'en, an' set her eyes to draw 'en. Oh, a saint she was! An' he, the poor shammick, went. 'Twas a good girl, you understand, that wished for to marry an' reform 'en. She had money, too. *I?* I'd ha' poured out my blood for 'en: that's all I cud do. So he went.

"As the place shines this day, it shone then. Like a moth it drew 'en. Late o' summer evenin's its windeys shone when down below here 'twas chill i' the hill's shadow. An' late at night the candles burned up there as he courted her. Purity and cosiness, you understand, an' down here—he forgot about down here. Before he'd missed to speak to me for a month, I'd hear 'en whistlin' up the hill, so merry as a grig. Well, he married her.

"They was married three months, an' 'twas harvest time come round, an' I in his vield a-gleanin'. For I was suffered near to that extent, seem' that the cottage here had been my fathers', an' was mine, an' out o't they culdn' turn me. One o' the hands, as they was pitchin', passes me an empty keg, an' says, 'Run you to the farm-place an' get it filled.' So with it I went to th' kitchen, and while I waited outside I sees his coat an' wesket 'pon a peg i' the passage. Well I knew the coat; an' a madness takin' me for all my loss, I unhitched it an' flung it behind the door, an', the keg bein' filled, picked it up agen and ran down home-along.

"No thought had I but to win Seth back. 'Twas the charm you spoke about: an' that same midnight I delved a hole by the dreshold an' buried the coat, whisperin', '*Man, come back, come back to me*!' as Aun' Lesnewth had a-taught me, times afore.

"But she, the pale woman, had a-seen me, dro' a chink o' the parlour-door, as I tuk the coat down. An' she knowed what I tuk it for. I've a-read it, times and again, in her wifely eyes; an' to-day you yoursel' are witness that she knowed. If Seth knowed—"

She clenched and unclenched her fist, and went on rapidly.

"Early next mornin', and a'most afore I was dressed, two constables came in by the gate, an' she behind 'em treadin' delicately, an' *he* at her back, wi' his chin dropped. They charged me wi' stealin' that coat—wi' stealin' it—that coat that I'd a-darned an' patched years afore ever *she* cuddled against its sleeve!"

"What happened?" I asked, as her voice sank and halted.

"What happened? She looked me i' the eyes scornfully; an' her own were full o' knowledge. An' wi' her eyes she coaxed and dared me to abase mysel' an' speak the truth an' win off jail. An' I, that had stole nowt, looked back at her an' said, 'It's true. I stole the coat. Now cart me off to jail; but handle me gently for the sake o' my child unborn.' When I spoke these last two words an' saw her face draw up wi' the bitterness o' their taste, I held out my wrists and clapped the handcuffs together like cymbals and laughed wi' a glad heart."

She caught my hand suddenly, and drawing me to the porch, pointed high above Sheba, to the yellow upland where the harvesters moved.

"Do 'ee see 'en there?—that tall young man by the hedge—there where the slope dips? That's my son, Seth's son, the straightest man among all. Neither spot has he, nor wart, nor blemish 'pon his body; and when she pays 'en his wages, Saturday evenin's, he says 'Thank 'ee, ma'am,' wi' a voice that's the very daps o' his father's. An' she's childless. Ah, childless woman! Childless woman! Go back an' carry word to her o' the prayer I've spoken upon her childlessness."

And "Childless woman!" "Childless woman!" she called twice again, shaking her fist at the windows of Sheba Farm-house, that blazed back angrily against the westering sun.

13

WHEN THE SAP ROSE.

A FANTASIA.

An old yellow van—the *Comet*—came jolting along the edge of the downs and shaking its occupants together like peas in a bladder. The bride and bridegroom did not mind this much; but the Registrar of Births, Deaths, and Marriages, who had bound them in wedlock at the Bible Christian Chapel two hours before, was discomforted by a pair of tight boots, that nipped cruelly whenever he stuck out his feet to keep his equilibrium.

Nevertheless, his mood was genial, for the young people had taken his suggestion and acquired a copy of their certificate. This meant five extra shillings in his pocket. Therefore, when the van drew up at the cross-roads for him to alight, he wished them long life and a multitude of children with quite a fatherly air.

"You can't guess where I'm bound for. It's to pay my old mother a visit. Ah, family life's the pretty life—that ever *I* should say it!"

They saw no reason why he should be cynical, more than other men. And the bride, in whose eyes this elderly gentleman with the tight boots appeared a rosy winged Cupid, waved her handkerchief until the vehicle had sidled round the hill, resembling in its progress a very infirm crab in a hurry.

As a fact, the Registrar wore a silk hat, a suit of black West-of-England broadcloth, a watch-chain made out of his dead wife's hair, and two large seals that clashed together when he moved. His face was wide and round, with a sanguine complexion, grey side-whiskers, and a cicatrix across the chin. He had shaved in a hurry that morning, for the wedding was early, and took place on the extreme verge of his district. His is a beautiful office—recording day by day the solemnest and most mysterious events in nature. Yet, standing at the cross-roads, between down and woodland, under an April sky full of sun and south-west wind, he threw the ugliest shadow in the landscape.

The road towards the coast dipped—too steeply for tight boots—down a wooded coombe, and he followed it, treading delicately. The hollow of the V ahead, where the hills overlapped against the pale blue, was powdered with a faint brown bloom, soon to be green—an infinity of bursting buds. The larches stretched their arms upwards, as men waking. The yellow was out on the gorse, with a heady scent like a pineapple's, and between the bushes spread the grey film of coming blue-bells. High up, the pines sighed along the ridge, turning paler; and far down, where the brook ran, a mad duet was going on between thrush and chaffinch—"*Cheer up, cheer up, Queen!*" "*Clip clip, clip, and kiss me—Sweet!*"—one against the other.

Now, the behaviour of the Registrar of Births, Deaths, and Marriages changed as he descended the valley. At first he went from side to side, because the loose stones were sharp and lay unevenly; soon he zig-zagged for another purpose—to peer into the bank for violets, to find a gap between the trees where, by bending down with a hand on each knee and his head tilted back, he could see the primroses stretching in broad sheets to the very edge of the pine-woods. By frequent tilting his collar broke from its stud and his silk hat settled far back on his neck. Next he unbuttoned his waistcoat and loosened his braces; but no, he could not skip—his boots were too tight. He looked at each tree as he passed. "If I could only see"—he muttered. "I'll swear there used to be one on the right, just here."

But he could not find it here—perhaps his memory misgave him—and presently turned with decision, climbed the low fence on his left, between him and the hollow of the coombe, and dropped into the plantation on the other side. Here the ground was white in patches with anemones; and as his feet crushed them, descending, the babel of the birds grew louder and louder.

He issued on a small clearing by the edge of the brook, where the grass was a delicate green, each blade pushing up straight as a spear-point from the crumbled earth. Here were more anemones, between patches of last year's bracken, and on the further slope a mass of daffodils. He pulled out a pocket-knife that had sharpened some hundreds of quill pens, and looking to his right, found what he wanted at once.

It was a sycamore, on which the buds were swelling. He cut a small twig, as big round as his middle finger, and sitting himself down on a barked log, close by, began to measure and cut it to a span's length, avoiding all knots. Then, taking the knife by the blade between finger and thumb, he tapped the bark gently with the tortoise-shell handle. And as he tapped, his face went back to boyhood again, in spite of the side-whiskers, and his mouth was pursed up to a silent tune.

For ten minutes the tapping continued; the birds ceased their contention, and broke out restlessly at intervals. A rabbit across the brook paused and listened at the funnel-shaped mouth of his hole, which caught the sound and redoubled it.

"Confound these boots!" said the Registrar, and pulling them off, tossed them among the primroses. They were "elastic-sides."

The tapping ceased. A breath of the land-ward breeze came up, combing out the tangle that winter had made in the grass, caught the brook on the edge of a tiny fall, and puffed it back six inches in a spray of small diamonds. It quickened the whole copse. The oak-saplings rubbed their old leaves one on another, as folks rub their hands, feeling life and warmth; the chestnut-buds groped like an infant's fingers; and the chorus broke out again, the thrush leading—"*Tiurru, tiurru, chippewee; tio-tee, tio-tee; queen, queen, que-een*!"

In a moment or two he broke off suddenly, and a honey-bee shot out of an anemone-bell like a shell from a mortar. For a new sound disconcerted them—a sound sharp and piercing. The Registrar had finished his whistle and was blowing like mad, moving his fingers up and down. Having proved his instrument, he dived a hand into his tail-pocket and drew out a roll, tied around with ribbon. It was the folded leather-bound volume in which he kept his blank certificates. And spreading it on his knees, he took his whistle again and blew, reading his music from the blank pages, and piping a strain he had never dreamed of. For he whistled of Births and Marriages.

O, happy Registrar! O, happy, happy Registrar! You will never get into those elastic-sides again. Your feet swell as they tap the swelling earth, and at each tap the flowers push, the sap climbs, the speck of life moves in the hedge-sparrow's egg; while, far away on the downs, with each tap, the yellow van takes bride and groom a foot nearer felicity. It is hard work in worsted socks, for you smite with the vehemence of Pan, and Pan had a hoof of horn.

* * * * *

The Registrar's mother lived in the fishing-village, two miles down the coombe. Her cottage leant back against the cliff so closely, that the boys, as they followed the path above, could toss tabs of turf down her chimney: and this was her chief annoyance.

Now, it was close on the dinner-hour, and she stood in her kitchen beside a pot of stew that simmered over the wreck-wood fire.

Suddenly a great lump of earth and grass came bouncing down the chimney, striking from side to side, and soused into the pot, scattering the hot stew over the hearth-stone and splashing her from head to foot.

Quick as thought, she caught up a besom and rushed out around the corner of the cottage.

"You stinking young adders!" she began.

A big man stood on the slope above her.

"Mother, cuff my head, that's a dear. I couldn' help doin' it."

It was the elderly Registrar. His hat, collar, tie, and waistcoat were awry; his boots were slung on the walking-stick over his shoulder; stuck in his mouth and lit was a twist of root-fibre, such as country boys use for lack of cigars, and he himself had used, forty years before.

The old woman turned to an ash-colour, leant on her besom, and gasped.

"William Henry!"

"I'm not drunk, mother: been a Band of Hope these dozen years." He stepped down the slope to her and bent his head low. "Box my ears, mother, quick! You used to have a wonderful gift o' cuffin'."

"William Henry, I'm bound to do it or die."

"Then be quick about it."

Half-laughing, half-sobbing, she caught him a feeble cuff, and next instant held him close to her old breast. The Registrar disengaged himself after a minute, brushed his eyes, straightened his hat, picked up the besom, and offered her his arm. They passed into the cottage together.

THE PAUPERS

I.

[Greek: ou men gar tou ge kreisson kai areion, ae hoth homophroneonte noaemasin oikon echaeton anaer aede gunae.]

Round the skirts of the plantation, and half-way down the hill, there runs a thick fringe of wild cherry-trees. Their white blossom makes, for three weeks in the year, a pretty contrast with the larches and Scotch firs that serrate the long ridge above; and close under their branches runs the line of oak rails that marks off the plantation from the meadow.

16

A labouring man came deliberately round the slope, as if following this line of rails. As a matter of fact, he was treading the little-used footpath that here runs close alongside the fence for fifty yards before diverging down-hill towards the village. So narrow is this path that the man's boots were powdered to a rich gold by the buttercups they had brushed aside.

By-and-bye he came to a standstill, looked over the fence, and listened. Up among the larches a faint chopping sound could just be heard, irregular but persistent. The man put a hand to his mouth, and hailed—

"Hi-i-i! Knock off! Stable clock's gone noo-oon!"

Came back no answer. But the chopping ceased at once; and this apparently satisfied the man, who leaned against the rail and waited, chewing a spear of brome-grass, and staring steadily, but incuriously, at his boots. Two minutes passed without stir or sound in this corner of the land. The human figure was motionless. The birds in the plantation were taking their noonday siesta. A brown butterfly rested, with spread wings, on the rail—so quietly, he might have been pinned there.

A cracked voice was suddenly lifted a dozen yards off, and within the plantation—

"Such a man as I be to work! Never heard a note o' that blessed clock, if you'll believe me. Ab-sorbed, I s'pose."

A thin withered man in a smock-frock emerged from among the cherry-trees with a bill-hook in his hand, and stooped to pass under the rail.

"Ewgh! The pains I suffer in that old back of mine you'll never believe, my son, not till the appointed time when you come to suffer 'em yoursel'. Well-a-well! Says I just now, up among the larches, 'Heigh, my sonny-boys, I can crow over you, anyways; for I was a man grown when Squire planted ye; and here I be, a lusty gaffer, markin' ye down for destruction.' But hullo! where's the dinner?"

"There bain't none."

"Hey?"

"There bain't none."

"How's that? Damme! William Henry, dinner's dinner, an' don't you joke about it. Once you begin to make fun o' sacred things like meals and vittles—"

"And don't you flare up like that, at your time o' life. We're fashionists to-day: dining out. 'Quarter after nine this morning I was passing by the Green wi' the straw-cart, when old Jan Trueman calls after me, 'Have 'ee heard the news?' What news?' says I. 'Why,' says he, 'me an' my missus be going into the House this afternoon—can't manage to pull along by ourselves any more,' he says; 'an' we wants you an' your father to drop in soon after noon an' take a bite wi' us, for old times' sake. 'Tis our last taste o' free life, and we'm going to do the thing fittywise,' he says."

The old man bent a meditative look on the village roofs below.

"We'll pleasure 'en, of course," he said slowly. "So 'tis come round to Jan's turn? But a' was born in the year of Waterloo victory, ten year' afore me, so I s'pose he've kept his doom off longer than most."

The two set off down the footpath. There is a stile at the foot of the meadow, and as he climbed it painfully, the old man spoke again.

"And his doorway, I reckon, 'll be locked for a little while, an' then opened by strangers; an' his nimble youth be forgot like a flower o' the field; an' fare thee well, Jan Trueman! Maria, too—I can mind her well as a nursing mother—a comely woman in her day. I'd no notion they'd got this in their mind."

"Far as I can gather, they've been minded that way ever since their daughter Jane died, last fall."

From the stile where they stood they could look down into the village street. And old Jan Trueman was plain to see, in clean linen and his Sunday suit, standing in the doorway and welcoming his guests.

"Come ye in—come ye in, good friends," he called, as they approached. "There's cold bekkon, an' cold sheep's liver, an' Dutch cheese, besides bread, an' a thimble-full o' gin-an'-water for every soul among ye, to make it a day of note in the parish."

He looked back over his shoulder into the kitchen. A dozen men and women, all elderly, were already gathered there. They had brought their own chairs. Jan's wife wore her bonnet and shawl, ready to start at a moment's notice. Her luggage in a blue handkerchief lay on the table. As she moved about and supplied her guests, her old lips twitched nervously; but when she spoke it was with no unusual tremor of the voice.

"I wish, friends, I could ha' cooked ye a little something hot; but there'd be no time for the washing-up, an' I've ordained to leave the place tidy."

One of the old women answered—

"There's nought to be pardoned, I'm sure. Never do I mind such a gay set-off for the journey. For the gin-an'-water is a little addition beyond experience. The vittles, no doubt, you begged up at the Vicarage, sayin' you'd been a peck o' trouble to the family, but this was going to be the last time."

"I did, I did," assented Mr. Trueman.

"But the gin-an'-water—how on airth you contrived it is a riddle!"

The old man rubbed his hands together and looked around with genuine pride.

"There was old Miss Scantlebury," said another guest, a smock-frocked gaffer of seventy, with a grizzled shock of hair. "You remember Miss Scantlebury?"

"O' course, o' course."

"Well, she did it better 'n anybody I've heard tell of. When she fell into redooced circumstances she sold the eight-day clock that was the only thing o' value she had left. Brown o' Tregarrick made it, with a very curious brass dial, whereon he carved a full-rigged ship that rocked like a cradle, an' went down stern foremost when the hour struck. 'Twas worth walking a mile to see. Brown's grandson bought it off Miss Scantlebury for two guineas, he being proud of his grandfather's skill; an' the old lady drove into Tregarrick Work'us behind a pair o' greys wi' the proceeds. Over and above the carriage hire, she'd enough left to adorn the horse wi' white favours an' give the rider a crown, large as my lord. Aye, an' at the Work'us door she said to the fellow, said she, 'All my life I've longed to ride in a bridal chariot; an' though my only lover died of a decline when I was scarce twenty-two, I've done it at last,' said she; 'an' now heaven an' airth can't undo it!'"

A heavy silence followed this anecdote, and then one or two of the women vented small disapproving coughs. The reason was the speaker's loud mention of the Workhouse. A week, a day, a few-hours before, its name might have been spoken in Mr. and Mrs. Trueman's presence. But now they had entered its shadow; they were "going"—whether to the dim vale of Avilion, or with chariot and horses of fire to heaven, let nobody too curiously ask. If Mr. and Mrs. Trueman chose to speak definitely, it was another matter.

Old Jan bore no malice, however, but answered, "That beats me, I own. Yet we shall drive, though it be upon two wheels an' behind a single horse. For Farmer Lear's driving into Tregarrick in an hour's time, an' he've a-promised us a lift."

"But about that gin-an'-water? For real gin-an'-water it is, to sight an' taste."

"Well, friends, I'll tell ye: for the trick may serve one of ye in the days when you come to follow me, tho' the new relieving officer may have learnt wisdom before then. You must know we've been considering of this step for some while, but hearing that old Jacobs was going to retire soon, I says to Maria, 'We'll bide till the new officer comes, and if he's a green hand, we'll diddle 'en.' Day before yesterday,' as you, was his first round at the work; so I goes up an' draws out my ha'af-crown same as usual, an' walks straight off for the Four Lords for a ha'af-crown's worth o' gin. Then back I goes, an' demands an admission order for me an' the missus. 'Why, where's your ha'af-crown?' says he. 'Gone in drink,' says I. 'Old man,' says he, 'you'm a scandal, an' the sooner you're put out o' the way o' drink, the better for you an' your poor wife.' 'Right you are,' I says; an' I got my order. But there, I'm wasting time; for to be sure you've most of ye got kith and kin in the place where we'm going, and 'll be wanting to send 'em a word by us."

* * * * *

It was less than an hour before Farmer Lear pulled up to the door in his red-wheeled spring-cart.

"Now, friends," said Mrs. Trueman, as her ears caught the rattle of the wheels, "I must trouble ye to step outside while I tidy up the floor."

The women offered their help, but she declined it. Alone she put the small kitchen to rights, while they waited outside around the door. Then she stepped out with her bundle, locked the door after her, and slipped the key under an old flower-pot on the window ledge. Her eyes were dry.

"Come along, Jan."

There was a brief hand-shaking, and the paupers climbed up beside Farmer Lear.

"I've made a sort o' little plan in my head," said old Jan at parting, "of the order in which I shall see ye again, one by one. 'Twill be a great amusement to me, friends, to see how the fact fits in wi' my little plan."

The guests raised three feeble cheers as the cart drove away, and hung about for several minutes after it had passed out of sight, gazing along the road as wistfully as more prosperous men look in through churchyard gates at the acres where their kinsfolk lie buried.

II.

The first building passed by the westerly road as it descends into Tregarrick is a sombre pile of some eminence, having a gateway and lodge before it, and a high encircling wall. The sun lay warm on its long roof, and the slates flashed gaily there, as Farmer Lear came over the knap of the hill and looked down on it. He withdrew his eyes nervously to glance at the old couple beside him. At the same moment he reined up his dun-coloured mare.

"I reckoned," he said timidly, "I reckoned you'd be for stopping hereabouts an' getting down. You'd think it more seemly—that's what I reckoned: an' 'tis down-hill now all the way."

For ten seconds and more neither the man nor the woman gave a sign of having heard him. The spring-cart's oscillatory motion seemed to have entered into their spinal joints; and now that they had come to a halt, their heads continued to wag forward and back as they contemplated the haze of smoke spread, like a blue scarf over the town, and the one long slate roof that rose from it as if to meet them. At length the old woman spoke, and with some viciousness, though her face remained as blank as the Workhouse door.

"The next time I go back up this hill, if ever I do, I'll be carried up feet first."

"Maria," said her husband, feebly reproachful, "you tempt the Lord, that you do."

"Thank 'ee, Farmer Lear," she went on, paying no heed; "you shall help us down, if you've a mind to, an' drive on. We'll make shift to trickly 'way down so far as the gate; for I'd be main vexed if anybody that had known me in life should see us creep in. Come along, Jan."

Farmer Lear alighted, and helped them out carefully. He was a clumsy man, but did his best to handle them gently. When they were set on their feet, side by side on the high road, he climbed back, and fell to arranging the reins, while he cast about for something to say.

"Well, folks, I s'pose I must be wishing 'ee good-bye." He meant to speak cheerfully, but over-acted, and was hilarious instead. Recognising this, he blushed.

"We'll meet in heaven, I daresay," the woman answered. "I put the door-key, as you saw, under the empty geranium-pot 'pon the window-ledge; an' whoever the new tenant's wife may be, she can eat off the floor if she's minded. Now drive along, that's a good soul, and leave us to fend for ourselves."

They watched him out of sight before either stirred. The last decisive step, the step across the Workhouse threshold, must be taken with none to witness. If they

20

could not pass out of their small world by the more reputable mode of dying, they would at least depart with this amount of mystery. They had left the village in Farmer Lear's cart, and Farmer Lear had left them in the high road; and after that, nothing should be known.

"Shall we be moving on?" Jan asked at length. There was a gate beside the road just there, with a small triangle of green before it, and a granite roller half-buried in dock-leaves. Without answering, the woman seated herself on this, and pulling a handful of the leaves, dusted her shoes and skirt.

"Maria, you'll take a chill that'll carry you off, sitting 'pon that cold stone."

"I don't care. 'Twon't carry me off afore I get inside, an' I'm going in decent, or not at all. Come here, an' let me tittivate you."

He sat down beside her, and submitted to be dusted.

"You'd as lief lower me as not in their eyes, I verily believe."

"I always was one to gather dust."

"An' a fresh spot o' bacon-fat 'pon your weskit, that I've kept the moths from since goodness knows when!"

Old Jan looked down over his waistcoat. It was of good "West-of-England broadcloth, and he had worn it on the day when he married the woman at his side.

"I'm thinking—" he began.

"Hey?"

"I'm thinking I'll find it hard to make friends in—in there. 'Tis such a pity, to my thinking, that by reggilations we'll be parted so soon as we get inside. You've a-got so used to my little ways an' corners, an' we've a-got so many little secrets together an' old-fash'ned odds an' ends o' knowledge, that you can take my meaning almost afore I start to speak. An' that's a great comfort to a man o' my age. It'll be terrible hard, when I wants to talk, to begin at the beginning every time. There's that old yarn o' mine about Hambly's cow an' the lawn-mowing machine—I doubt that anybody 'll enjoy it so much as you always do; an' I've so got out o' the way o' telling the beginning—which bain't extra funny, though needful to a stranger's understanding the whole joke—that I 'most forgets how it goes."

"We'll see one another now an' then, they tell me. The sexes meet for Chris'mas-trees an' such-like."

"I'm jealous that 'twon't be the same. You can't hold your triflin' confabs with a great Chris'mas-tree blazin' away in your face as important as a town afire."

"Well, I'm going to start along," the old woman decided, getting on her feet; "or else someone 'll be driving by and seeing us."

Jan, too, stood up.

"We may so well make our congees here," she went on, "as under the porter's nose."

An awkward silence fell between them for a minute, and these two old creatures, who for more than fifty years had felt no constraint in each other's presence, now looked into each other's eyes with a fearful diffidence. Jan cleared his throat, much as if he had to make a public speech.

"Maria," he began in an unnatural voice, "we're bound for to part, and I can trewly swear, on leaving ye, that—"

"—that for two-score year and twelve It's never entered your head to consider whether I've made 'ee a good wife or a bad. Kiss me, my old man; for I tell 'ee I wouldn' ha' wished it other. An' thank 'ee for trying to make that speech. What did it feel like?"

"Why, 't rather reminded me o' the time when I offered 'ee marriage."

"It reminded me o' that, too. Com'st along."

They tottered down the hill towards the Workhouse gate. When they were but ten yards from it, however, they heard the sound of wheels on the road behind them, and walked bravely past, pretending to have no business at that portal. They had descended a good thirty yards beyond (such haste was put into them by dread of having their purpose guessed) before the vehicle overtook them—a four-wheeled dog-cart carrying a commercial traveller, who pulled up and offered them a lift into the town.

They declined.

Then, as soon as he passed out of sight, they turned, and began painfully to climb back towards the gate. Of the two, the woman had shown the less emotion. But all the way her lips were at work, and as she went she was praying a prayer. It was the only one she used night and morning, and she had never changed a word since she learned it as a chit of a child. Down to her seventieth year she had never found it absurd to beseech God to make her "a good girl"; nor did she find it so as the Workhouse gate opened, and she began a new life.

CUCKOO VALLEY RAILWAY

This century was still young and ardent when ruin fell upon Cuckoo Valley. Its head rested on the slope of a high and sombre moorland, scattered with granite and china-clay; and by the small town of Ponteglos, where it widened out into arable and grey pasture-land, the Cuckoo river grew deep enough to float up vessels of small tonnage from the coast at the spring tides. I have seen there the boom of a trading schooner brush the grasses on the river-bank as she came before a southerly wind, and the haymakers stop and almost crick their necks staring up at her top-sails. But between the moors and Ponteglos the valley wound for fourteen miles or so between secular woods, so steeply converging that for the most part no more room was left at the bottom of the V than the river itself filled. The fisherman beside it trampled on pimpernels, sundew, watermint, and asphodels, or pushed between clumps of *Osmunda regalis* that overtopped him by a couple of feet. If he took to wading, there was much ado to stand against the current. Only here and there it spread into a still black pool, greased with eddies; and beside such a pool, it was odds that he found a diminutive meadow, green and flat as a billiard-table, and edged with clumps of fern. To think of Cuckoo Valley is to call up the smell of that fern as it wrapped at the bottom of the creel the day's catch of salmon-peal and trout.

The town of Tregarrick (which possessed a gaol, a workhouse, and a lunatic asylum, and called itself the centre of the Duchy) stood three miles back from the lip of this happy valley, whither on summer evenings its burghers rambled to eat cream and junket at the Dairy Farm by the river bank, and afterwards sit to watch the fish rise, while the youngsters and maidens played hide-and-seek in the woods. But there came a day when the names of Watt and Stephenson waxed great in the land, and these slow citizens caught the railway frenzy. They took it, however, in their own fashion. They never dreamed of connecting themselves with other towns and a larger world, but of aggrandisement by means of a railway that should run from Tregarrick to nowhere in particular, and bring the intervening wealth to their doors. They planned a railway that should join Tregarrick with Cuckoo Valley, and there divide into two branches, the one bringing ore and clay from the moors, the other fetching up sand and coal from the sea. Surveyors and engineers descended upon the woods; then a cloud of navvies. The days were filled with the crash of falling timber and the rush of emptied trucks. The stream was polluted, the fish died, the fairies were evicted from their rings beneath the oak, the morals of the junketing houses underwent change. The vale knew itself no longer; its smoke went up week by week with the noise of pick-axes and oaths.

On August 13th, 1834, the Mayor of Tregarrick declared the new line open, and a locomotive was run along its rails to Dunford Bridge, at the foot of the moors. The engine was christened *The Wonder of the Age*; and I have before me a handbill of the festivities of that proud day, which tells me that the mayor himself rode in an open truck, "embellished with Union Jacks, lions and unicorns, and other loyal devices." And then Nature settled down to heal her wounds, and the Cuckoo Yalley Railway to pay no dividend to its promoters.

It is now two years and more since, on an August day, I wound up my line by Dunford Bridge, and sauntered towards the Light Horseman Inn, two gunshots up the road. The time was four o'clock, or thereabouts, and a young couple sat on a bench by the inn-door, drinking cocoa out of one cup. Above their heads and along the house-front a vine-tree straggled, but its foliage was too thin to afford a speck of shade as they sat there in the eye of the westering sun. The man (aged about one-and-twenty) wore the uncomfortable Sunday-best of a mechanic, with a shrivelled, but still enormous, bunch of Sweet-William in his buttonhole. The girl was dressed in a bright green gown and a white bonnet. Both were flushed and perspiring, and I still think they must have ordered hot cocoa in haste, and were repenting it at leisure. They lifted their eyes and blushed with a yet warmer red as I passed into the porch.

Two men were seated in the cool tap-room, each with a pasty and a mug of beer. A composition of sweat and coal-dust had caked their faces, and so deftly smoothed all distinction out of their features that it seemed at the moment natural and proper to take them for twins. Perhaps this was an error: perhaps, too, their appearance of extreme age was produced by the dark grey dust that overlaid so much of them as showed above the table. As twins, however, I remember them, and cannot shake off the impression that they had remained twins for an unusual number of years.

One addressed me. "Parties outside pretty comfortable?" he asked.

"They were drinking out of the same cup," I answered.

He nodded. "Made man and wife this mornin'. I don't fairly know what's best to do. Lord knows I wouldn' hurry their soft looks and dilly-dallyin'; but did 'ee notice how much beverage was left in the cup?"

"They was mated at Tregarrick, half-after-nine this mornin'," observed the other twin, pulling out a great watch, "and we brought 'em down here in a truck for their honeymoon. The agreement was for an afternoon in the woods; but by crum! sir, they've sat there and held one another's hand for up'ards of an hour after the stated time to start. And we ha'nt the heart to tell 'em so."

He walked across to the window and peered over the blind.

"There's a mort of grounds in the cocoa that's sold here," he went on, after a look, "and 'tisn't the sort that does the stomach good, neither. For their own sakes, I'll give the word to start, and chance their thankin' me some day later when they learn what things be made of."

The other twin arose, shook the crumbs off his trousers, and stretched himself. I guessed now that this newly-married pair had delayed traffic at the Dunford terminus of the Cuckoo Valley Railway for almost an hour and a half; and I determined to travel into Tregarrick by the same train.

So we strolled out of the inn towards the line, the lovers following, arm-in-arm, some fifty paces behind.

"How far is it to the station?" I inquired.

The twins stared at me.

Presently we turned down a lane scored with dry ruts, passed an oak plantation, and came on a clearing where the train stood ready. The line did not finish: it ended in a heap of sand. There were eight trucks, seven of them laden with granite, and an engine, with a prodigiously long funnel, bearing the name *The Wonder of the Age* in brass letters along its boiler.

"Now," said one of the twins, while the other raked up the furnace, "you can ride in the empty truck with the lovers, or on the engine along with us—which you like."

I chose the engine. We climbed on board, gave a loud whistle, and jolted oil. Far down, on our right, the river shone between the trees, and these trees, encroaching on the track, almost joined their branches above us. Ahead, the moss that grew upon the sleepers gave the line the appearance of a green glade, and the grasses, starred with golden-rod and mallow, grew tall to the very edge of the rails. It seemed that in a few more years Nature would cover this scar of 1834, and score the return match against man. Hails, engine, officials, were already no better than ghosts: youth, and progress lay in the pushing trees, the salmon leaping against the dam below, the young man and maid sitting with clasped hands and amatory looks in the hindmost truck.

At the end of three miles or so we gave an alarming whistle, and slowed down a bit. The trees were thinner here, and I saw that a high-road came down the hill, and cut across our track some fifty yards ahead. We prepared to cross it cautiously.

"Ho-o-oy! Stop!"

The brake was applied, and as we came to a standstill a party of men and women descended the hill towards us.

"'Tis Susan Warne's seventh goin' to be christen'd, by the look of it," said the engine-driver beside me; "an', by crum! we've got the Kimbly."

The procession advanced. In the midst walked a stout woman, carrying a baby in long clothes, and in front a man bearing in both hands a plate covered with a white cloth. He stepped up beside the train, and, almost before I had time to be astonished, a large yellow cake was thrust into my hands. Engine-driver and stoker were also presented with a cake apiece, and then the newly-married pair, who took and ate with some shyness and giggling.

"Is it a boy or a girl?" asked the stoker, with his mouth full.

"A boy," the man answered; "and I count it good luck that you men of modern ways should be the first we meet on our way to church. The child 'll be a go-ahead if there's truth in omens."

"You're right, naybour. We're the speediest men in this part of the universe, I d' believe. Here's luck to 'ee, Susan Warne!" he piped out, addressing one of the women; "an' if you want a name for your seventh, you may christen 'en after the engine here, the *Wonder of the Age*."

We waved our hats and jolted off again towards Tregarrick. At the end of the journey the railway officials declined to charge for the pleasure of my company. But after some dispute, they agreed to compromise by adjourning to the Railway Inn, and drinking prosperity to Susan Warne's seventh.

THE CONSPIRACY ABOARD THE *MIDAS*.

"Are you going home to England? So am I. I'm Johnny; and I've never been to England before, but I know all about it. There's great palaces of gold and ivory—that's for the lords and bishops—and there's Windsor Castle, the biggest of all, carved out of a single diamond—that's for the queen. And she's the most beautiful lady in the whole world, and feeds her peacocks and birds of paradise out of a ruby cup. And there the sun is always shining, so that nobody wants any candles. O, words would fail me if I endeavoured to convey to you one-half of the splendours of that enchanted realm!"

This last sentence tumbled so oddly from the childish lips, that I could not hide a smile as I looked down on my visitor. He stood just outside my cabin-door—a small serious boy of about eight, with long flaxen curls hardly dry from his morning bath. In the pauses of conversation he rubbed his head with a big bath-towel. His legs and feet were bare, and he wore only a little shirt and velveteen breeches, with scarlet ribbons hanging untied at the knees.

"You're laughing!"

I stifled the smile.

"What were you laughing at?"

"Why, you're wrong, little man, on just one or two points," I answered evasively.

"Which?"

"Well, about the sunshine in England. The sun is not always shining there, by any means."

"I'm afraid you know very little about it," said the boy, shaking his head.

"Johnny! Johnny!" a voice called down the companion-ladder at this moment. It was followed by a thin, weary-looking man, dressed in carpet slippers and a suit of seedy black. I guessed his age at fifty, but suspect now that the lines about his somewhat prim mouth were traced there by sorrows rather than by years. He bowed to me shyly, and addressed the boy.

"Johnny, what are you doing here? in bare feet!"

"Father, here is a man who says the sun doesn't always shine in England."

The man gave me a fleeting embarrassed glance, and echoed, as if to shirk answering—

"In bare feet!"

"But it does, doesn't it? Tell him that it does," the child insisted.

Driven thus into a corner, the father turned his profile, avoiding my eyes, and said dully—

"The sun is always shining in England."

"Go on, father; tell him the rest."

"—and the use of candles, except as a luxury, is consequently unknown to the denizens of that favoured clime," he wound up, in the tone of a man who repeats an old, old lecture.

Johnny was turning to me triumphantly, when his father caught him by the hand and led him back to his dressing. The movement was hasty, almost rough. I stood at the cabin-door and looked after them.

We were fellow-passengers aboard the *Midas*, a merchant barque of near on a thousand tons, homeward bound from Cape Town; and we had lost sight of the Table Mountain but a couple of days before. It was the first week of the new year, and all day long a fiery sun made life below deck insupportable. Nevertheless, though we three were the only passengers on board, and lived constantly in sight of each other, it was many days before I made any further acquaintance with Johnny and his father. The sad-faced man clearly desired to avoid me, answering my nod with a cold embarrassment, and clutching Johnny's hand whenever the child called "Good-morning!" to me cordially. I fancied him ashamed of his foolish falsehood; and I, on my side, was angry because of it. The pair were for ever strolling backwards and forwards on deck, or resting beneath the awning on the poop, and talking—always talking. I fancied the boy was delicate; he certainly had a bad cough during the first few days. But this went away as our voyage proceeded, and his colour was rich and rosy.

One afternoon I caught a fragment of their talk as they passed, Johnny brightly dressed and smiling, his father looking even more shabby and weary than usual. The man was speaking.

"And Queen Victoria rides once a year through the streets of London on her milk-white courser, to hear the nightingales sing in the Tower. For when she came to the throne the Tower was full of prisoners, but with a stroke of her sceptre she changed them all into song-birds. Every year she releases fifty; and that is why they sing so rapturously, because each one hopes his turn has come at last."

I turned away. It was unconscionable to cram the child's mind with these preposterous fables. I pictured the poor little chap's disappointment when the bleak reality came to stare him in the face. To my mind, his father was worse than an idiot, and I could hardly bring myself to greet him next morning, when we met.

My disgust did not seem to trouble him. In a timid way, even, his eyes expressed satisfaction. For a week or two I let him alone, and then was forced to speak.

It happened in this way. We had spun merrily along the tail of the S.E. trades and glided slowly to a standstill on a glassy ocean, and beneath a sun that at noon left us shadowless. A fluke or two of wind had helped us across the line; but now, in 2° 27' north latitude, the *Midas* slept like a turtle on the greasy sea. The heat of the near African coast seemed to beat like steam against our faces. The pitch bubbled like caviare in the seams of the white deck, and the shrouds and ratlines ran with tears of tar. To touch the brass rail of the poop was to blister the hand, to catch a whiff from the cook's galley was to feel sick for ten minutes. The hens in their coops lay with eyes glazed and gasped for air. If you hung forward over the bulwarks you stared down into your own face. The sailors grumbled and cursed and panted as they huddled forward under a second awning that was rigged up to give them shade rather than coolness; for coolness was not to be had.

On the second afternoon of the calm I happened to pass this awning, and glanced in. Pretty well all the men were there, lounging, with shirts open and chests streaming with sweat; and in their midst on a barrel, sat Johnny, with a flushed face.

The boatswain—Gibbings by name—was speaking. I heard him say—"An' the Lord Mayor 'll be down to meet us, sonny, at the docks, wi' his five-an'-fifty black boys all ablowin' blowin' Hallelujarum on their silver key-bugles. An' we'll be took in tow to the Mansh'n 'Ouse an' fed—" here he broke off and passed the back of his hand across his mouth, with a glance at the ship's cook, who had been driven from his galley by the heat. But the cook had no suggestions to make. His soul was still sick with the reek of the boiled pork and pease pudding he had cooked two hours before under a torrid and vertical sun.

"We'll put it at hokey-pokey, nothin' a lump, if you *don't* mind, sonny," the boatswain went on; "in a nice airy parlour painted white, with a gilt chandelier an' gilt combings to the wainscot." His picture of the Mansion House as he proceeded was drawn from his reading in the Book of Revelations and his own recollections of Thames-side gin-palaces and the saloons of passenger steamers, and gave the impression of a virtuous gambling-hell. The whole crew listened admiringly, and it seemed they were all in the stupid conspiracy. I resolved, for Johnny's sake, to protest, and that very evening drew Gibbings aside and expostulated with him.

"Why," I asked, "lay up this cruel, this certain disappointment for the little chap? Why yarn to him as if he were bound for the New Jerusalem?"

The boatswain stared at me point-blank, at first incredulously, then with something like pity.

"Why, sir, don't you know? Can't you see for yoursel'? It's because he *is* bound for the New Jeroosalem; because—bless his tender soul!—that's all the land he'll ever touch."

"Good Lord!" I cried. "Nonsense! His cough's better; and look at his cheeks."

"Ay—we knows that colour on this line. His cough's better, you say; and I say this weather's killing him. You just wait for the nor'-east trades."

I left Gibbings, and after pacing up and down the deck a few times, stepped to the bulwarks, where a dark figure was leaning and gazing out over the black waters. Johnny was in bed; and a great shame swept over me as I noted the appealing wretchedness of this lonely form.

I stepped up and touched him softly on the arm.

"Sir, I am come to beg your forgiveness."

Next morning I joined the conspiracy.

After his father, I became Johnny's most constant companion. "Father disliked you at first," was the child's frank comment; "he said you told fibs, but now he wants us to be friends." And we were excellent friends. I lied from morning to night—lied glibly, grandly. Sometimes, indeed, as I lay awake in my berth, a horror took me lest the springs of my imagination should run dry. But they never did. As a liar, I out-classed every man on board.

But by-and-bye, as we caught the first draught of the trades, the boy began to punctuate my fables with that hateful cough. This went on for a week; and one day, in the midst of our short stroll, his legs gave way under him. As I caught him in my arms, he looked up with a smile.

"I'm very weak, you know. But it'll be all right when I get to England."

But it was not till we had passed well beyond the equatorial belt that Johnny grew visibly worse. In a week he had to lie still on his couch beneath the awning, and the patter of his feet ceased on the deck. The captain, who was a bit of a doctor, said to me one day—

"He will never live to see England."

But he did.

It was a soft spring afternoon when the *Midas* sighted the Lizard, and Johnny was still with us, lying on his couch, though almost too weak to move a limb. As the day wore on we lifted him once or twice to look.

28

"Can you see them quite plain?" he asked; "and the precious stones hanging on the trees? And the palaces—and the white elephants?"

I stared through my glass at the serpentine rocks and white-washed lighthouse above them, all powdered with bronze and gold by the sinking sun, and answered—

"Yes, they are all there."

All that afternoon we were beside him, looking out and peopling the shores of home with all manner of vain shows and pageants; and when one man broke down another took his place.

As the sun fell, and twilight drew on, the bright revolving lights on the two towers suddenly flashed out their greeting. We were about to carry the child below, for the air was chilly; but he saw the flash, and held up a feeble hand.

"What is that?"

"Those two lights," I answered, telling my final lie, "are the lanterns of Cormelian and Cormoran, the two Cornish giants. They'll be standing on the shore to welcome us. See—each swings his lantern round, and then for a moment it is dark; now wait a moment, and you'll see the light again."

"Ah!" said the child, with a smile and a little sigh, "it is good to be—home!"

And with that word on his lips, as he waited for the next flash, Johnny stretched himself and died.

LEGENDS OF ST. PIRAN.

I.—SAINT PIRAN AND THE MILLSTONE.

Should you visit the Blackmore tin-streamers on their feast-day, which falls on Friday-in-Lide (that is to say, the first Friday in March), you may note a truly Celtic ceremony. On that day the tinners pick out the sleepiest boy in the neighbourhood and send him up to the highest *bound* in the works, with instructions to sleep there as long as he can. And by immemorial usage the length of his nap will be the measure of the tinners' afternoon siesta for twelve months to come.

Now, this first week in March is St. Piran's week: and St. Piran is the miners' saint. To him the Cornishmen owe not only their tin, which he discovered on the spot, but also their divine laziness, which he brought across from Ireland and naturalised here. And I learned his story one day from an old miner, as we ate our bread and cheese together on the floor of Wheal Tregobbin, while the Davy lamp between us made wavering giants of our shadows on the walls of the adit, and the sea moaned as it tossed on its bed, two hundred feet above.

* * * * *

St. Piran was a little round man; and in the beginning he dwelt on the north coast of Ireland, in a leafy mill, past which a stream came tumbling down to the sea. After turning the saint's mill-wheel, the stream dived over a fall into the Lough below, and the *lul-ul-ur-r-r* of the water-wheel and fall was a sleepy music in the saint's ear noon and night.

It must not be imagined that the mill-wheel ground anything. No; it went round merely for the sake of its music. For all St. Piran's business was the study of objects that presented themselves to his notice, or, as he called it, the "Rapture av Contemplation"; and as for his livelihood, he earned it in the simplest way. The waters of the Lough below possessed a peculiar virtue. You had only to sink a log or stick therein, and in fifty years' time that log or stick would be turned to stone. St. Piran was as quick as you are to divine the possibilities of easy competence offered by this spot. He took time by the forelock, and in half a century was fairly started in business. Henceforward he passed all his days among the rocks above the fall, whistling to himself while he whittled bits of cork and wood into quaint shapes, attached them to string, weighted them with pebbles, and lowered them over the fall into the Lough— whence, after fifty years he would draw them forth, and sell them to the simple surrounding peasantry at two hundred and fifty *per centum per annum* on the initial cost.

It was a tranquil, lucrative employment, and had he stuck to the Rapture of Contemplation, he might have ended his days by the fall. But in an unlucky hour he undertook to feed ten Irish kings and their armies for three weeks anend on three cows. Even so he might have escaped, had he only failed. Alas! As it was, the ten kings had no sooner signed peace and drunk together than they marched up to St. Piran's door, and began to hold an Indignation Meeting.

"What's ailing wid ye, then?" asked the saint, poking his head out at the door; "out wid ut! Did I not stuff ye wid cow-mate galore when the land was as nakud as me tonshure? But 'twas three cows an' a miracle wasted, I'm thinkin'."

"Faith, an' ye've said ut!" answered one of the kings. "Three cows between tin Oirish kings! 'Tis insultin'! Arrah, now, make it foive, St. Piran darlint!"

"Now may they make your stummucks ache for that word, ye marautherin' thieves av the world!"

And St. Piran slammed the door in their faces.

But these kings were Ulstermen, and took things seriously. So they went off and stirred up the people: and the end was that one sunshiny morning a dirty rabble marched up to the mill and laid hands on the saint. On what charge, do you think? Why, for *Being without Visible Means of Support!*

"There's me pethrifyin' spicimins!" cried the saint: and he tugged at one of the ropes that stretched down into the Lough.

"Indade!" answered one of the ten kings: "Bad luck to your spicimins!" says he.

"Fwhat's that ye're tuggin.' at?" asks a bystander.

"Now the Holy Mother presarve your eyesight, Tim Coolin," answers St. Piran, pulling it in, "if ye can't tell a plain millstone at foive paces! I never asked ye to see *through* ut," he added, with a twinkle, for Tim had a plentiful lack of brains, and that the company knew.

Sure enough it was a millstone, and a very neat one; and the saint, having raised a bit of a laugh, went on like a cheap-jack:

30

"Av there's any gintleman prisunt wid an eye for millstones, I'll throuble him to turn ut here. Me own make," says he, "jooled in wan hole, an' dog-chape at fifteen shillin'—"

He was rattling away in this style when somebody called out, "To think av a millstone bein' a visible means av support!" And this time the laugh turned against the saint.

"St. Piran dear, ye've got to die," says the spokesman.

"Musha, musha!"—and the saint set up a wail and wrung his hands. "An' how's it goin' to be?" he asked, breaking off; "an' if 'tis by Shamus O'Neil's blunderbust that he's fumblin' yondther, will I stand afore or ahint ut? for 'tis fatal both ends, I'm thinkin', like Barney Sullivan's mule. Wirra, wirra! May our souls find mercy, Shamus O'Neil, for we'll both, be wantin' ut this day. Better for you, Shamus, that this millstone was hung round your black neck, an' you drownin' in the dept's av the Lough!"

The words were not spoken before they all set up a shout. "The millstone! the millstone!" "Sthrap him to ut!" "He's named his death!"—and inside of three minutes there was the saint, strapped down on his own *specimen*.

"Wirra, wirra!" he cried, and begged for mercy; but they raised a devastating shindy, and gave the stone a trundle. Down the turf it rolled and rolled, and then *whoo!* leaped over the edge of the fall into space and down—down—till it smote the waters far below, and knocked a mighty hole in them, and went under—

For three seconds only. The next thing that the rabble saw as they craned over the cliff was St. Piran floating quietly out to sea on the millstone, for all the world as if on a life-belt, and untying his bonds to use for a fishing-line! You see, this millstone had been made of cork originally, and was only half petrified; and the old boy had just beguiled them. When he had finished undoing the cords, he stood up and bowed to them all very politely.

"Visible Manes av Support, me childher—merely Visible Manes av Support!" he called back.

'Twas a sunshiny day, and while St. Piran chuckled the sea twinkled all over with the jest. As for the crowd on the cliff, it looked for five minutes as if the saint had petrified them harder than the millstone. Then, as Tim Coolin told his wife, Mary Dogherty, that same evening, they dispersed promiscuously in groups of one each.

Meanwhile, the tides were bearing St. Piran and his millstone out into the Atlantic, and he whiffed for mackerel all the way. And on the morrow a stiff breeze sprang up and blew him sou'-sou'-west until he spied land; and so he stepped ashore on the Cornish coast.

In Cornwall he lived many years till he died: and to this day there are three places named after him—Perranaworthal, Perranuthno and Perranzabuloe. But it was in the last named that he took most delight, because at Perranzabuloe (Perochia Sti. Pirani in Sabulo) there was nothing but sand to distract him from the Study of Objects that Presented Themselves to his Notice: for he had given up miracles. So he sat on the sands and taught the Cornish people how to be idle. Also he discovered tin for them; but that was an accident.

A full fifty years had St. Piran dwelt among the sandhills between Perranzabuloe and the sea before any big rush of saints began to pour into Cornwall: for 'twas not till the old man had discovered tin for us that they sprang up thick as blackberries all over the county; so that in a way St. Piran had only himself to blame when his idle ways grew to be a scandal by comparison with the push and bustle of the newcomers.

Never a notion had he that, from Rome to Land's End, all his holy brethren were holding up their hands over his case. He sat in his cottage above the sands at Perranzabuloe and dozed to the hum of the breakers, in charity with all his parishioners, to whom his money was large as the salt wind; for his sleeping partnership in the tin-streaming business brought him a tidy income. And the folk knew that if ever they wanted religion, they had only to knock and ask for it.

But one fine morning, an hour before noon, the whole parish sprang to its feet at the sound of a horn. The blast was twice repeated, and came from the little cottage across the sands.

"'Tis the blessed saint's cow-horn!" they told each other. "Sure the dear man must be in the article of death!" And they hurried off to the cottage, man, woman, and child: for 'twas thirty years at least since the horn had last been sounded.

They pushed open the door, and there sat St. Piran in his arm-chair, looking good for another twenty years, but considerably flustered. His cheeks were red, and his fingers clutched the cow-horn nervously.

"Andrew Penhaligon," said he to the first man that entered, "go you out and ring the church bell."

Off ran Andrew Penhaligon. "But, blessed father of us," said one or two, "we're all *here*! There's no call to ring the church bell, seem' you're neither dead nor afire, blessamercy!"

"Oh, if you're all here, that alters the case; for 'tis only a proclamation I have to give out at present. To-morrow mornin'—Glory be to God!—I give warnin' that Divine service will take place in the parish church."

"You're sartin you bain't feelin' poorly, St. Piran dear?" asked one of the women.

"Thank you, Tidy Mennear, I'm enjoyin' health. But, as I was sayin', the parish church 'll be needed to-morrow, an' so you'd best set to and clean out the edifice: for I'm thinkin'," he added, "it'll be needin' that."

"To be sure, St. Piran dear, we'll humour ye."

"'Tisn' that at all," the saint answered; "but I've had a vision."

"Don't you often?"

"H'm! but this was a peculiar vision; or maybe a bit of a birdeen whispered it into my ear. Anyway, 'twas revealed to me just now in a dream that I stood on the lawn at Bodmin Priory, and peeped in at the Priory window. An' there in the long hall sat all the saints together at a big table covered with red baize and plotted against us. There was St. Petroc in the chair, with St. Guron by his side, an' St. Neot, St. Udy, St. Teath, St. Keverne, St. Wen, St. Probus, St. Enodar, St. Just, St. Fimbarrus, St. Clether, St. Germoe, St. Veryan, St. Winnock, St. Minver, St. Anthony, with the virgins Grace, and Sinara, and Iva—the whole passel of 'em. An' they were agreein' there was no holiness left in this parish of mine; an' speakin' shame of me, my childer—of me, that have banked your consciences these fifty years, and always been able to pay on demand: the more by token that I kept a big reserve, an' you knew it. Answer me: when was there ever a panic in Perranzabuloe? "Twas all very well,' said St. Neot, when his turn came to speak, 'but this state o' things ought to be exposed.' He's as big as bull's beef, is St. Neot, ever since he worked that miracle over the fishes, an' reckons he can disparage an old man who was makin' millstones to float when he was suckin' a coral. But the upshot is, they're goin' to pay us a Visitation to-morrow, by surprise. And, if only for the parish credit, we'll be even wid um, by dad!"

St. Piran still lapsed into his native brogue when strongly excited.

But he had hardly done when Andrew Penhaligon came running in—

"St. Piran, honey, I've searched everywhere; an' be hanged to me if I can find the church at all!"

"Fwhat's become av ut?" cried the saint, sitting up sharply.

"How should I know? But devil a trace can I see!"

"Now, look here," St. Piran said; "the church was there, right enough."

"That's a true word," spoke up an old man, "for I mind it well. An elegant tower it had, an' a shingle roof."

"Spake up, now," said the saint, glaring around; "fwich av ye's gone an' misbestowed me parush church? For I won't believe," he said, "that it's any worse than carelussness—at laste, not yet-a-bit."

Some remembered the church, and some did not: but the faces of all were clear of guilt. They trooped out on the sands to search.

Now, the sands by Perranzabuloe are for ever shifting and driving before the northerly and nor'-westerly gales; and in time had heaped themselves up and covered the building out of sight. To guess this took the saint less time than you can wink your eye in; but the bother was that no one remembered exactly where the church, had stood, and as there were two score at least of tall mounds along the shore, and all of pretty equal height, there was no knowing where to dig. To uncover them all was a job to last till doomsday.

"Blur-an'-agurs, but it's ruined I am!" cried St. Piran. "An' the Visitashun no further away than to-morra at tin a.m.!" He wrung his hands, then caught up a spade, and began digging like a madman.

They searched all day, and with lanterns all the night through: they searched from Ligger Point to Porth Towan: but came on never a sign of the missing church.

"If it only had a spire," one said, "there'd be some chance." But as far as could be recollected, the building had a dumpy tower.

"Once caught, twice shy," said another; "let us find it this once, an' next time we'll have landmarks to dig it out by."

It was at sunrise that St. Piran, worn-out and heart-sick, let fall his spade and spoke from one of the tall mounds, where he had been digging for an hour.

"My children," he began, and the men uncovered their heads, "my children, we are going to be disgraced this day, and the best we can do is to pray that we may take it like men. Let us pray."

He knelt down on the great sand-hill, and the men and women around dropped on their knees also. And then St. Piran put up the prayer that has made his name famous all the world over.

_THE PRAYER OF ST. PIRAN.

Harr us, O Lord, and be debonair: for ours is a particular case. We are not like the men of St. Neot or the men of St. Udy, who are for ever importuning Thee upon the least occasion, praying at all hours and every day of the week. Thou knowest it is only with extreme cause that we bring ourselves to trouble Thee. Therefore regard our moderation in time past, and be instant to help us now. Amen_.

There was silence for a full minute as he ceased; and then the kneeling parishioners lifted their eyes towards the top of the mound.

St. Piran was nowhere to be seen!

They stared into each other's faces. For a while not a sound was uttered. Then a woman began to sob—

"We've lost 'en! We've lost 'en!"

"Like Enoch, he's been taken!"

"Taken up in a chariot an' horses o' fire. Did any see 'en go?"

"An' what'll we do without 'en? Holy St. Piran, come back to us!"

"Hullo! hush a bit an' hearken!" cried Andrew Penhaligon, lifting a hand.

They were silent, and listening as he commanded, heard a muffled voice and a faint, calling as it were from the bowels of the earth.

"Fetch a ladder!" it said: "fetch a ladder! It's meself that's found ut, glory be to God! Holy queen av heaven! but me mouth is full av sand, an' it's burstin' I'll be if ye don't fetch a ladder quick!"

They brought a ladder and set it against the mound. Three of the men climbed up. At the top they found a big round hole, from the lip of which they scraped the sand away, discovering a patch of shingle roof, through which St. Piran— whose weight had increased of late—had broken and tumbled heels over head into his own church.

Three hours later there appeared on the eastern sky-line, against the yellow blaze of the morning, a large cavalcade that slowly pricked its way over the edge and descended the slopes of Newlyn Downs. It was the Visitation. In the midst rode St. Petroc, his crozier tucked under his arm, astride a white mule with scarlet ear-tassels and bells and a saddle of scarlet leather. He gazed across the sands to the sea, and turned to St. Neot, who towered at his side upon a flea-bitten grey.

"The parish seems to be deserted," said he: "not a man nor woman can I see, nor a trace of smoke above the chimneys."

St. Neot tightened his thin lips. In his secret heart he was mightily pleased.

"Eight in the morning," he answered, with a glance back at the sun. "They'll be all abed, I'll warrant you."

St. Petroc muttered a threat.

They entered the village street. Not a soul turned out at their coming. Every cottage door was fast closed, nor could any amount of knocking elicit an answer or entice a face to a window. In gathering wrath the visiting saints rode along the sea-shore to St. Piran's small hut.

Here the door stood open: but the hut was empty. A meagre breakfast of herbs was set out on the table, and a brand new scourge lay somewhat ostentatiously beside the platter. The visitors stood nonplussed, looked at each other, then eyed the landscape. Between barren sea and barren downs the beach stretched away, with not a human shape in sight. St. Petroc, choking with impotent wrath, appeared to study the hollow green breakers from between the long ears of his mule, but with quick sidelong glances right and left, ready to jump down the throat of the first saint that dared to smile.

After a minute or so St. Enodar suddenly turned his face inland, and held up a finger.

"Hark!" he shouted above the roar of the sea.

"What is it?"

"It sounds to me," said St. Petroc, after listening for some moments with his head on one side, "it sounds to me like a hymn."

"To be sure 'tis a hymn," said St. Enodar, "and the tune is 'Mullyon,' for a crown." And he pursed up his lips and followed the chant, beating time with his forefinger—

When, like a thief, the Midianite
Shall steal upon the camp,
O, let him find our armour bright,
And oil within our lamp!"

"But where in the world does it come from?" asked St. Neot.

This could not be answered for the moment; but the saints turned their horses' heads from the sea, and moved slowly on the track of the sound, which at every step grew louder and more distinct.

"*It is at no appointed hours,*
It is not by the dock,
That Satan, grisly wolf, devours
The unprotected flock"

The visitors found themselves at the foot of an enormous sand-hill, from the top of which the chant was pouring as lava from a crater. They set their ears to the sandy wall. They walked round it, and listened again.

35

"But ever prowls th' insidious foe,
And listens round the fold"

This was too much. St. Petroc smote twice upon the sand-hill with his crozier, and shouted—

"Hi, there!"

The chant ceased. For at least a couple of minutes nothing happened; and then St. Piran's bald head was thrust cautiously forward over the summit.

"Holy St. Petroc! Was it only you, after all? And St. Neot—and St. Udy O, glory be!"

"Why, who did you imagine we were?" St. Petroc asked, still in amazement.

"Why, throat-cutting Danes, to be sure, by the way you were comin' over the hills when we spied you, three hours back. An' the trouble we've had to cover up our blessed church out o' sight of thim maraurtherin' thieves! An' the intire parish gathered inside here an' singin' good-by songs in expectation of imminent death! An' to think 'twas you holy men, all the while! But why didn't ye send word ye was comin', St. Petroc, darlint? For it's little but sand ye'll find in your mouths for breakfast, I'm thinkin'."

IN THE TRAIN.

I.—PUNCH'S UNDERSTUDY.

The first-class smoking compartment was the emptiest in the whole train, and even this was hot to suffocation, because my only companion denied me more than an inch of open window. His chest, he explained curtly, was "susceptible." As we crawled westward through the glaring country, the sun's rays reverberated on the carriage roof till I seemed to be crushed under an anvil, counting the strokes. I had dropped my book, and was staring listlessly out of the window. At the other end of the compartment my fellow-passenger had pulled down the blinds, and hidden his face behind the *Western Morning News*. He was a red and choleric little man of about sixty, with a protuberant stomach, a prodigious nose, to which he carried snuff about once in two minutes, and a marked deformity of the shoulders. For comfort—and also, perhaps, to hide this hump—he rested his back in the angle by the window. He wore a black alpaca coat, a high stock, white waistcoat, and trousers of shepherd's plaid. On these and a few other trivial details I built a lazy hypothesis that he was a lawyer, and unmarried.

Just before entering the station at Lostwithiel, our train passed between the white gates of a level crossing. A moment before I had caught sight of the George drooping from the church spire, and at the crossing I saw it was regatta-day in the small town. The road was thick with people and lined with sweet-standings; and by the near end of the bridge a Punch-and-Judy show had just closed a performance. The orchestra had unloosed his drum, and fallen to mopping the back of his neck with the red handkerchief that had previously bound the panpipes to his chin. A crowd still loitered around, and among it I noted several men and women in black—ugly stains upon the pervading sunshine.

The station platform was cram-full as we drew up, and it was clear at once that all the carriages in the train would be besieged, without regard to class. By some chance, however, ours was neglected, and until the very last moment we seemed likely to escape. The guard's whistle was between his lips when I heard a shout, then one or two feminine screams, and a company of seven or eight persons came charging out of the booking-office. Every one of them was apparelled in black: they were, in fact, the people I had seen gaping at the Punch-and-Judy show.

In a moment one of the men tore open the door of our compartment, and we were invaded. One—two—four—six—seven—in they poured, tumbling over my legs, panting, giggling inanely, exhorting each other to hurry—an old man, two youths, three middle-aged women, and a little girl about four years old. I heard a fierce guttural sound, and saw my fellow-passenger on his feet, choking with wrath and gesticulating. But the guard slammed the door on his resentment, and the train moved on. As it gathered speed he fell back, all purple above his stock, snatched his malacca walking-cane from under the coat-tails of a subsiding youth, stuck it upright between his knees, and glared round upon the intruders. They were still possessed with excitement over their narrow escape, and unconscious of offence. One of the women dropped into the corner seat, and took the little girl on her lap. The child's dusty boots rubbed against the old gentleman's trousers. He shifted his position, grunted, and took snuff furiously.

"That was nibby-jibby," observed the old man of the party, while his eyes wandered round for a seat.

"I declare I thought I should ha' died," panted a robust-looking woman with a wart on her cheek, and a yard of crape hanging from her bonnet. "Can't 'een find nowhere to sit, uncle?"

"Reckon I must make shift 'pon your lap, Susannah."

This was said with a chuckle, and the woman tittered.

"What new-fang'd game be this o' the Great Western's? Arms to the seats, I vow. We'll have to sit intimate, my dears."

"'Tis First Class," one of the young men announced in a chastened whisper: "I saw it written on the door."

There was a short silence of awe.

"Well!" ejaculated Susannah: "I thought, when first I sat down, that the cushions felt extraordinary plum. You don't think they'll fine us?"

"It all comes of our stoppin' to gaze at that Punch-an'-Judy," the old fellow went on, after I had shown them how to turn back the arm-seats, and they were settled in something like comfort. "But I never *could* refrain from that antic, though I feels condemned too, in a way, an' poor Thomas laid in earth no longer ago than twelve noon. But in the midst of life we are in death."

"I don't remember a more successful buryin'," said the woman who held the little girl.

"That was partly luck, as you may say, it bein' regatta-day an' the fun o' the fair not properly begun. I counted a lot at the cemetery I didn' know by face, an' I set 'em down for excursionists, that caught sight of a funeral, an' followed it to fill up the time."

"It all added."

"Oh, aye; Thomas was beautifully interred."

By this time the heat in the carriage was hardly more overpowering than the smell of crape, broadcloth, and camphor. The youth who had wedged himself next to me carried a large packet of "fairing," which he had bought at one of the sweet-stalls. He began to insert it into his side pocket, and in his struggles drove an elbow sharply into my ribs. I shifted my position a little.

"Tom's wife would ha' felt it a source o' pride, had she lived."

But I ceased to listen; for in moving I had happened to glance at the further end of the carriage, and there my attention was arrested by a curious little piece of pantomime. The little girl—a dark-eyed, intelligent child, whose pallor was emphasised by the crape which smothered her—was looking very closely at the old gentleman with the hump—staring at him hard, in fact. He, on the other hand, was leaning forward, with both hands on the knob of his malacca, his eyes bent on the floor and his mouth squared to the surliest expression. He seemed quite unconscious of her scrutiny, and was tapping one foot impatiently on the floor.

After a minute I was surprised to see her lean forward and touch him gently on the knee.

He took no notice beyond shuffling about a little and uttering a slight growl. The woman who held her put out an arm and drew back the child's hand reprovingly. The child paid no heed to this, but continued to stare. Then in another minute she again bent forward, and tapped the old gentleman's knee.

This time she fetched a louder growl from him, and an irascible glare. Not in the least daunted, she took hold of his malacca, and shook it to and fro in her small hand.

"I wish to heavens, madam, you'd keep your child to yourself!"

"For shame, Annie!" whispered the poor woman, cowed by his look.

But again Annie paid no heed. Instead, she pushed the malacca towards the old gentleman, saying—

"Please, sir, will 'ee warm Mister Barrabel wi' this?"

He moved uneasily, and looked harshly at her without answering. "For shame, Annie!" the woman murmured a second time; but I saw her lean back, and a tear started and rolled down her cheek.

"If you please, sir," repeated Annie, "will 'ee warm Mister Barrabel wi' this?"

The old gentleman stared round the carriage. In his eyes you could read the question, "What in the devil's name does the child mean?" The robust woman read it there, and answered him huskily—

"Poor mite! she's buried her father this mornin'; an' Mister Barrabel is the coffin-maker, an' nailed 'en down."

"Now," said Annie, this time eagerly, "will 'ee warm him same as the big doll did just now?"

Luckily, the old gentleman did not understand this last allusion. He had not seen the group around the Punch-and-Judy show; nor, if he had, is it likely he would have guessed the train of thought in the child's mind. But to me, as I looked at my fellow-passenger's nose and the deformity of his shoulders, and remembered how Punch treats the undertaker in the immortal drama, it was all plain enough. I glanced at the child's companions. Nothing in their faces showed that they took the allusion; and the next moment I was glad to think that I alone knew what had prompted Annie's speech.

For the next moment, with a beautiful change on his face, the old gentleman had taken the child on his knee, and was talking to her as I dare say he had never talked before.

"Are you her mother?" he asked, looking up suddenly, and addressing the woman opposite.

"Her mother's been dead these two year. I'm her aunt, an' I'm takin' her home to rear 'long wi' my own childer."

He was bending over Annie, and had resumed his chat. It was all nonsense— something about the silver knob of his malacca—but it took hold of the child's fancy and comforted her. At the next station I had to alight, for it was the end of my journey. But looking back into the carriage as I shut the door, I saw Annie bending forward over the walking-stick, and following the pattern of its silverwork with her small finger. Her face was turned from the old gentleman's, and behind her little black hat his eyes were glistening.

II.—A CORRECTED CONTEMPT.

The whistles had sounded, and we were already moving slowly out of St. David's Station, Exeter, to continue our journey westward, when the door was pulled open and a brown bag, followed by a whiff of *Millefleurs* and an over-dressed young man, came flying into the compartment where I sat alone and smoked.

The youth scrambled to a seat as the door slammed behind him; remarked that it was "a near shave"; and laughed nervously as if to assure me that he found it a joke. His face was pink with running, and the colour contrasted unpleasantly with his pale sandy hair and moustache. He wore a light check suit, a light-blue tie knotted through a "Mizpah" ring, a white straw hat with a blue ribbon, and two finger-rings set with sham diamonds—altogether the sort of outfit that its owner would probably have described as "rather nobby." Feeling that just now it needed a few repairs, he opened the bag, pulled out a duster and flicked away for half-a-minute at his brown boots. Next with a handkerchief he mopped his face and wiped round the inner edge first of his straw hat, and then of his collar and cuffs. After this he stood up, shook his trousers till they hung with a satisfying gracefulness, produced a cigar-case—covered with forget-me-nots in crewel work—and a copy of the *Sporting Times*, sat down again, and asked me if I could oblige him with a light.

I think the train had neared Dawlish before the cigar was fairly started, and his pink face hidden behind the pink newspaper. But even so between the red sandstone cliffs and the wholesome sea this pink thing would not sit still. His diamond rings kept flirting round the edge of the *Sporting Times*, his brown boots shifting their position on the cushion in front of him, his legs crossing, uncrossing, recrossing, his cigar-smoke rising in quick, uneasy puffs.

Between Teignmouth and Newton Abbot this restlessness increased. He dropped some cigar-ash on his waistcoat and arose to shake it off. Twice or thrice he picked up the paper and set it down again. As we ran into Newton Abbot Station, he came over to my side of the carriage and scanned the small crowd upon the platform. Suddenly his pink cheeks flushed to crimson. The train was slowing to a standstill, and while he hesitated with a hand on the door, a little old man came trotting down the platform—a tremulous little man, in greenish black broadcloth, eloquent of continued depression in some village retail trade. His watery eyes shone brimful of pride and gladness.

"Whai, Charley, lad, there you be, to be shure; an' lookin' as peart as a gladdy! Shaäke your old vather's vist, lad—ees fay, you be lookin' well!"

The youth, scorched with a miserable shame, stepped out, put his hand in his father's, and tried to withdraw him a little up the platform and out of my hearing.

"Noa, noa; us'll bide where us be, zoa's to be 'andy vur the train when her starts off. Her doan't stay no while. I vound Zam Emmet zarving here as porter—you mind Zam? Danged if I knawed 'en, vurst along, the vace of 'en's that altered: grawed a beard, her hev. But her zays to me, 'How be gettin' 'long, Isaac?' an' then I zaw who 'twas—an' us fell to talkin', an' her zaid the train staps vaive minnits, no more nor less."

His son interrupted him with mincing haughtiness.

"'Ow's mothaw?"

"Weist an' ailin', poor crittur—weist an' ailin'. Dree times her've a-been through the galvanic battery, an' might zo well whistle. Turble lot o' zickness about. An' old Miss Ruby's resaigned, an' a new postmistress come in her plaäce—a tongue-tight pore crittur, an' talks London. If you'll b'lieve *me*, Miss Ruby's been to Plymouth 'pon her zavings an' come back wi' vifteen pound' worth of valse teeth in her jaws, which, as I zaid, 'You must excoose my plain speakin', but they've a-broadened your mouth, Miss Ruby, an' I laiked 'ee better as you was bevore.' 'Never mind,' her zays, 'I can chow.' There now, Charley— zimme I've been doing arl the tarlk, an' thy mother'll be waitin' wi' dree-score o' questions, zoon as I gets whome. Her'd ha' corned to gie thee a kiss, if her'd a-been 'n a vit staäte; but her's zent thee zummat—"

He foraged in the skirt pockets of his threadbare coat and brought out a paper of sandwiches and a long-nosed apple. I saw the young man wince.

"Her reckoned you'd veel a wamblin' in the stommick, travellin' arl the waäy from Hexeter to Plymouth. There, stow it awaäy. Not veelin' peckish? Never maind: there's a plenty o' taime betwix' this an' Plymouth."

"No, thanks."

"Tut-tut, now—" He insisted, and the packet, on the white paper wrapper of which spots of grease were spreading, changed hands. The little man peered wistfully up into his son's face: his own eyes were full of love, but seemed to search for something.

"How dost laike it, up to Hexeter: an' how't get along?"

"Kepital—kepital. Give mothaw my love."

"E'es be shure. Fainely plaized her'll be to hear thee'rt zo naicely adrest. Her'd maäde up her maind, pore zowl, that arl your buttons ud be out, wi' nobody to zee arter 'en. But I declare thee'rt drest laike a topsawyer."

And with this a dead silence fell between the two. The old man shifted his weight from one foot to another, and twice cleared his throat. The young counter-jumper averted his eyes from his father's quivering lip to stare up the platform. The minutes ran on.

At last the old man found his voice—

"Thic' there's a stubbard apple you've got in your hand."

"Take your seats, please!"

The guard held the door while they shook hands again. "Charley" leaned out at the window as our train began to move.

"Her comes from the zeccond 'spalier past the inyon-bed; al'ays the vurst to raipen, thic' there tree."

The old fellow broke into something resembling a run as he followed our carriage to shout—

"Turble bad zayson vur zaider!"

With that he halted at the end of the platform, and watched us out of sight. His son flung himself on the seat with—I could have kicked him for it—a deprecatory titter. Then he drew a long breath; but it was twenty minutes before his blush faded, and he regained confidence to ask me for another light.

Just eighteen months after I was travelling up to London in the Zulu express. A large Fair Trade meeting had been held at Plymouth the night before, and three farmers in the compartment with me were discussing that morning's leader in the *Western Daily Mercury*. One of them had already been goaded into violent speech when we halted at Newton Abbot and another passenger stepped in—a little old man in a suit of black.

I recognised him at once. And yet he was changed woefully. He had fallen away in flesh; the lines had deepened beside his upper lip; and in spite of a glossier suit he had an appearance of hopelessness which he had not worn when I saw him for the first time.

He took his seat, looked about him vacantly and caught the eye of the angry farmer, who nodded, broke off his speech in the middle of a sentence, and asked in a curiously gentle voice—

"Travellin' up to Exeter?"

The old man bent his head for "yes," and I saw the tears well up in his weak eyes.

"There's no need vur to ax your arrand." The farmer here dropped his tone almost to a whisper.

41

"Naw, naw. I be goin' up to berry 'en. Ees, vriends," he went on, looking around and asking, with that glance, the sympathy of all present, "to berry my zon, my clever zon, my only zon."

Nobody spoke for a few seconds. Then the kindly farmer observed—

"Aye, I've heerd zay a' was very clever to his traäde. 'Uxtable an' Co., his employers, spoke very handsome of 'en, they tell me. I can't call to maind, tho', that I've a-zet eyes 'pon the young man since he was a little tacker."

The old man began to fumble in his breastpocket, and drawing out a photograph, handed it across.

"That's the last that was took of 'en."

"Pore young chap," said the farmer, holding the likeness level with his eyes and studying it; "Pore young chap! Zuch a respectable lad to look at! They tell me a' made ye a gude zon, too."

"Gude?" The tears ran down the father's face and splashed on his hands, trembling as they folded over the knob of his stout stick. "Gude? I b'lieve, vriends, ye'll call it gude when a young man zends the third o' his earnin's week by week to help his parents. That's what my zon did, vrum the taime he left whome. An' presunts—never a month went by, but zome little gift ud come by the postman; an' little 'twas he'd got to live 'pon, at the best, the dear lad—"

The farmer was passing back the photograph. "May I see it?" I asked: and the old man nodded.

It was the same face—the same suit, even—that had roused my contempt eighteen months before.

WOON GATE.

It was on a cold and drenching afternoon in October that I spent an hour at Woon Gate: for in all the homeless landscape this little round-house offers the only shelter, its windows looking east and west along the high-road and abroad upon miles of moorland, hedgeless, dotted with peat-ricks, inhabited only by flocks of grey geese and a declining breed of ponies, the chartered vagrants of Woon Down. Two miles and more to the north, and just under the rim of the horizon, straggle the cottages of a few tin-streamers, with their backs to the wind. These look down across an arable country, into which the women descend to work at seed-time and harvest, and whence, returning, they bring some news of the world. But Woon Gate lies remoter. It was never more than a turnpike; and now the gate is down, the toll-keeper dead, and his widow lives alone in the round-house. She opened the door to me—a pleasant-faced old woman of seventy, in a muslin cap, red turnover, and grey gown hitched very high. She wore no shoes inside her cottage, but went about in a pair of coarse worsted stockings on all days except the very rawest, when the chill of the lime-ash floor struck into her bones.

"May I wait a few minutes till the weather lifts?" I asked.

She smiled and seemed almost grateful.

"You'm kindly welcome, be sure: that's if you don't mind the Vaccination."

I suppose that my face expressed some wonder: for she went on, shaking my dripping hat and hanging it on a nail by the fire—

"Doctor Rodda'll be comin' in half-an-hour's time. 'Tis district Vaccination to-day, and he always inoculates here, 'tis so handy."

She nodded her head at half a dozen deal chairs and a form arrayed round the wall under a row of sacred texts and tradesmen's almanacks.

"There'll be nine to-day, as I makes it out. I counted 'em up several times last night."

It was evidently a great day in her eyes.

"But you've allowed room for many more than nine," I pointed out.

"Why, of course. There's some brings their elder childer for a treat—an' there's always 'Melia Penaluna."

I was on the point of asking who Amelia Penaluna might be, when my attention was drawn to the small eastern window. Just outside, and but a dozen paces from the house, there stretched a sullen pond, over which the wind drove in scuds and whipped the sparse reeds that encroached around its margin. Beside the further bank of the pond the high-road was joined by a narrow causeway that led down from the northern fringe of Woon Down; and along this causeway moved a procession of women and children.

They were about twenty in all, and, as they skirted the pond, their figures were sharply silhouetted against the grey sky. Each of the women held a baby close to her breast and bent over it as she advanced against the wind, that beat her gown tightly against her legs and blew it out behind in bellying folds. Yet beneath their uncouth and bedraggled garments they moved like mothers of a mighty race, tall, large-limbed, broad of hip, hiding generous breasts beneath the shawls—red, grey, and black—that covered their babes from the wind and rain. A few of the children struggled forward under rickety umbrellas; but the mothers had their hands full, and strode along unsheltered. More than one, indeed, faced the storm without bonnet or covering for the head; and all marched along the causeway like figures on some sculptured frieze, their shadows broken beneath them on the ruffled surface of the pond. I said that each of the women carried a babe: but there was one who did not—a plain, squat creature, at the tail of the procession, who wore a thick scarf round her neck, and a shawl of divers bright colours. She led a small child along with one hand, and with the other attempted to keep a large umbrella against the wind.

"Nineteen—twenty—twenty-one," counted the toll-keeper's widow behind me as I watched the spasmodic jerkings of this umbrella. "I wasn't far out in my reckon. And you, sir, make twenty-two. It niver rains but it pours, they say. Times enow I don't see a soul for days together, not to hail by name, an' now you drops in on top of a Vaccination."

Her sigh over this plethora of good fortune was interrupted by a knocking at the door, and the mothers trooped in, their clothes dripping pools of water on the sanded lime-ash. One or two of them, after exchanging greetings with their hostess, bade me Good-morning: others eyed me in silence as they took their seats round the wall. All whose babes were not sound asleep quietly undid their bodices and began to give them suck. The older children scrambled into chairs and sat kicking their heels and tracing patterns on the floor with the water that ran off their umbrellas. They were restless but rather silent, as if awed by the shadow of the coming Vaccination. The woman who had brought up the procession, found a place in the far corner, and began to unwind the comforter around her neck. Her eyes were brighter and more agitated than any in the room.

"A brave trapse all the way from Upper Woon," remarked the youngest mother, wiping a smear of rain from her baby's forehead.

"Ah, 'tis your first, Mary Polsue. Wait till you've carried twelve such loads, my dear," said a tall middle-aged woman, whose black hair, coarse as a mane, was powdered grey with, raindrops.

"Dear now, Ellen; be this the twelfth?" our hostess exclaimed. "I was reckonin' it the 'leventh."

"Ay, th' twelfth—tho' I've most lost count. I buried one, you know."

"For my part," put in a pale-eyed blonde, who sat near the door, "'t seems but yestiddy I was here with Alsia yonder." She nodded her head towards a girl of five who was screwing herself round in her chair and trying to peep out of the window.

"Ay, they come and come: the Lord knows wherefore," the tall woman assented. "When they'm young they make your arms ache, an' when they grow up they make your heart ache."

"But 'Melia Penaluna's been here more times than any of us," said the blonde with a titter, directing her eyes towards a corner of the room. The rest looked too, and laughed. Turning, I saw that the plain-faced woman had unwound her comforter, and now I could see, hanging low on her chest, an immense lump wrapped in clean white linen and bound up with a gaudy yellow handkerchief. It was a goître.

"Iss, my dears," she answered, touching it and smiling, but with tears in her eyes; "this here's my only child, an' iver will be. Ne'er a man'll look 'pon me, so I'm forced to be content wi' this babe and clothe 'en pretty, as you see. Ah, you'm lucky, you'm lucky, though you talk so!"

"She's terrible fond o' childer," said one of the women audibly, addressing me. "How many 'noculations have you 'tended, 'Melia?"

"Six-an'-twenty, countin' to-day," 'Melia announced with pride in her trembling voice. But at this point one of the infants began to cry, and before he could be hushed the noise of wheels sounded down the road, and Dr. Rodda drove up in his reedy gig.

He was a round, dapper practitioner, with slightly soiled cuffs and an extremely business-like manner. On entering the room he jerked his head in a general nod to all present, and stepping to the table, drew a small packet from his waistcoat, and unfolded it. It contained about a score of small pieces of ivory, pointed like pens, but flat. Then, pulling out a paper and consulting it hastily, he set to work, beginning with the child that lay on the blonde woman's lap, next to the door.

I looked around. The children were staring with wide, admiring eyes. Their mothers also watched, but listlessly, still suckling their babes as each waited its turn. Only 'Melia Penaluna winced and squeezed her hands together whenever a feeble wailing told that one of the vaccine points had made itself felt.

"Do 'ee think it hurts the poor mites?" the youngest mother asked.

"Not much, I reckon," answered the big woman.

Nevertheless her own child cried pitifully when its turn came. And as it cried, the childless woman in the corner got off her chair and ran forward tremulously.

"'Becca, let me take him. Do'ee, co!"

"'Melia Penaluna, you'm no better 'n a fool."

But poor, misnamed Amelia was already back in her corner with the child, hugging it, kissing it, rocking it in her arms, crooning over it, holding it tightly against the lump that hung down on her barren bosom. Long after the baby had ceased to cry she sat crooning and yearning over it. And the mothers watched her, with wonder and scornful amusement in their eyes.

FROM A COTTAGE IN GANTICK.

I.—THE MOURNER'S HORSE.

The Board Schoolmaster and I are not friends. He is something of a zealot, and conceives it his mission to weed out the small superstitions of the countryside and plant exact information in their stead. He comes from up the country—a thin, clean-shaven town-bred man, whose black habit and tall hat, though considerably bronzed, refuse to harmonise with the scenery amid which they move. His speech is formal and slightly dogmatic, and in argument he always gets the better of me. Therefore, feeling sure it will annoy him excessively, I am going to put him into this book. He laid himself open the other day to this stroke of revenge, by telling me a story; and since he loves precision, I will be very precise about the circumstances.

At the foot of my garden, and hidden from my window by the clipt box hedge, runs Sanctuary Lane, along which I see the heads of the villagers moving to church on Sunday mornings. But in returning they invariably keep to the raised footpath on the far side, that brings the women's skirts and men's smallclothes into view. I have made many attempts to discover how this distinction arose, and why it is adhered to, but never found a satisfying explanation. It is the rule, however.

From the footpath a high bank (where now the primroses have given place to stitchwort and ragged robin) rises to an orchard; so steeply that the apple-blossom drops into the lane. Just now the petals lie thickly there in the early morning, to be trodden into dust as soon as the labourers fare to work. Beyond and above the orchard comes a stretch of pastureland and then a young oak-coppice, the fringe of a great estate, with a few Scotch firs breaking the sky-line on top of all. The head gamekeeper of this estate tells me we shall have a hot summer, because the oak this year was in leaf before the ash, though only by a day. The ash was foliating on the 29th of April, the oak on the 28th. Up there the blue-bells lie in sheets of mauve, and the cuckoo is busy. I rarely see him; but his three notes fill the hot noon and evening. When he spits (says the gamekeeper again) it is time to be sheep-shearing. My talk with the gamekeeper is usually held at six in the morning, when he comes down the lane and I am stepping across to test the water in Scarlet's Well.

This well bubbles up under a low vault scooped in the bank by the footpath and hung with hart's-tongue ferns. It has two founts, close together; but whereas one of them oozes only, the other is bubbling perennially, and, as near as I have observed, keeps always the same. Its specific gravity is that of distilled water— $1.000°$; and though, to be sure, it upset me, three weeks back, by flying up to $1.005°$, I think that must have come from the heavy thunderstorms and floods of rain that lately visited us and no doubt imported some ingredients that had no business there. As for its temperature, I will select a note or two of the observations I made with a Fahrenheit thermometer this last year:—

June 12th.—Temperature in shade of well, $62°$; of water, $51°$.

August 25th.—In shade of well (at noon), $73°$; of water, $52°$.

November 20th.—In shade of well, $43°$; of water, $52°$.

January 1st.—External air, $56°$; enclosure, $53°$; water, $52°$.

March 11th.—A bleak, sunless day. Temperature in shade of well, at noon, $54°$; water, $51°$. The *Chrysosplenium Oppositiflorium* in rich golden bloom within the enclosure.

But the spring has other properties besides its steady temperature. I was early abroad in my garden last Thursday week, and in the act of tossing a snail over my box hedge, when I heard some girls' voices giggling, and caught a glimpse of half-a-dozen sun-bonnets gathered about the well. Straightening myself up, I saw a group of maids from the village, and, in the middle, one who bent over the water. Presently she scrambled to her feet, glanced over her shoulder and gave a shrill scream.

I, too, looked up the lane and saw, a stone's throw off, the schoolmaster advancing with long and nervous strides. He was furiously angry.

"Thomasine Slade," said he, "you are as shameless as you are ignorant!"

The girl tossed her chin and was silent, with a warm blush on her cheek and a lurking imp of laughter in her eye. The schoolmaster frowned still more darkly.

"Shameless as well as ignorant!" he repeated, bringing the ferule of his umbrella smartly down upon the macadam; "and you, Jane Hewitt, and you, Lizzie Polkinghorne!"

"Why, what's the matter?" I asked, stepping out into the road.

At sight of me the girls broke into a peal of laughter, gathered up their skirts and fled, still laughing, down the road.

"What's the matter?" I asked again.

"The matter?" echoed the schoolmaster, staring blankly after the retreating skirts; then more angrily—"The matter? come and look here!" He took hold of my shirt-sleeve and led me to the well. Stooping, I saw half-a-dozen pins gleaming in its brown depths.

"A love-charm."

The schoolmaster nodded.

"Thomasine Slade has been wishing for a husband. I see no sin in that. When she looked up and saw you coming down the lane—"

I paused. The schoolmaster said nothing. He was leaning over the well, gloomily examining the pins.

"—your aspect was enough to scare anyone," I wound up lamely.

"I wish," the schoolmaster hastily began, "I wish to Heaven I had the gift of humour! I lose my temper and grow positive. I'd kill these stupid superstitions with ridicule, if I had the gift. It's a great gift. My God, I do hate to be laughed at!"

"Even by a fool?" I asked, somewhat astonished at his heat.

"Certainly. There's no comfort in comparing the laugh of fools with the crackling of thorns under a pot, if you happen to be inside the pot and in process of cooking."

He took off his hat, brushed it on the sleeve of his coat, and resumed in a tone altogether lighter—

"Yes, I hate to be laughed at; and I'll tell you a tale on this point that may amuse you at my expense.

"I am London-bred, as you know, and still a Cockney in the grain, though when I came down here to teach school I was just nineteen and now I'm over forty. It was during the summer holidays that I first set foot in this neighbourhood—a week before school re-opened. I came early, to look for lodgings and find out a little about the people and settle down a bit before beginning work.

"The vicar—the late vicar, I mean—commended me to old Retallack, who used to farm Rosemellin, up the valley, a widower and childless. His sister, Miss Jane Ann, kept house for him, and these were the only two souls on the premises till I came and was boarded by them for thirteen shillings a week. For that price they gave me a bedroom, a fair-sized sitting-room and as much as I could eat.

"A month after my arrival, Farmer Retallack was put to bed with a slight attack of colic. This was on a Wednesday, and on Saturday morning Miss Jane Ann came knocking at my door with a message that the old man would like to see me. So I went across to his room and found him propped up in the bed with three or four pillows and looking very yellow in the gills, though clearly convalescent.

"'Schoolmaster,' said he, 'I've a trifling favour to beg of ye. You give the children a half-holiday, Saturdays—hey? Well, d'ye think ye could drive the brown hoss, Trumpeter, into Tregarrick this afternoon? The fact is, my old friend Abe Walters, that kept the Packhorse Inn is lying dead, and they bury 'en at half after two to-day. I'd be main glad to show respect at the funeral and tell Mrs. Walters how much deceased 'll be missed, ancetera; but I might so well try to fly in the air. Now if you could attend and just pass the word that I'm on my back with the colic, but that you've come to show respect in my place, I'd take it very friendly of ye. There'll be lashins o' vittles an' drink. No Walters was ever interred under a kilderkin.'" Now the fact was, I had never driven a horse in my life and hardly knew (as they say) a horse's head from his tail till he began to move. But that is just the sort of ignorance no young man will readily confess to. So I answered that I was engaged that evening. We were just organising night-classes for the young men of the parish, and the vicar was to open the first, with a short address, at half-past six.

"'You'll be back in lashins o' time,' the farmer assured me.

"This put me fairly in a corner. 'To tell you the truth,' said I, 'I'm not accustomed to drive much.' But of course this was wickedly short of the truth.

"He declared that it was impossible to come to grief on the way, the brown horse being quiet as a lamb and knowing every stone of the road. And the end was that I consented. The brown horse was harnessed by the farm-boy and led round with the gig while Miss Jane Ann and I were finishing our midday meal. And I drove off alone in a black suit and with my heart in my mouth.

"Trumpeter, as the farmer had promised, was quiet as a lamb. He went forward at a steady jog, and even had the good sense to quarter on his own account for the one or two vehicles we met on the broad road. Pretty soon I began to experiment gingerly with the reins; and by the time we reached Tregarrick streets, was handling them with quite an air, while observing the face of everyone I met, to make sure I was not being laughed at. The prospect of Tregarrick Fore Street frightened me a good deal, and there was a sharp corner to turn at the entrance of the inn-yard. But the old horse knew his business so well that had I pulled on one rein with all my strength I believe it would have merely annoyed, without convincing, him. He took me into the yard without a mistake, and I gave up the reins to the ostler, thanking Heaven and looking careless.

"The inn was crowded with mourners, eating and drinking and discussing the dead man's virtues. They packed the Assembly Room at the back, where the subscription dances are held, and the reek of hot joints was suffocating. I caught sight of the widow Walters bustling up and down between the long tables and shedding tears while she changed her guests' plates. She heard my message, welcomed me with effusion, and thrusting a plateful of roast beef under my nose, hurried away to put on her bonnet for the funeral.

"A fellow on my right paused with his mouth full to bid me eat. 'Thank you,' I said, 'my only wish is to get out of this as quickly as possible.'

"He contemplated me for half a minute with an eye like an ox's; remarked 'You'll be a furriner, no doubt;' and went on with his meal.

"If the feasting was long, the funeral was longer. We sang so many burying-tunes, and the widow so often interrupted the service to ululate, that the town clock had struck four when I hurried back from the churchyard to the inn, and told the ostler to put my horse in the gig. I had little time to spare.

"'Beg your pardon, sir,' the ostler said, 'but I'm new to this place—only came here this day week. Which is your horse?'

"'Oh,' I answered, 'he's a brown. Make haste, for I'm in a hurry.'

"He went off to the stables and returned in about two minutes.

"'There's six brown hosses in the stable, sir. Would you mind coming and picking out yours?'

"I followed him with a sense of impending evil. Sure enough there were six brown horses in the big stable, and to save my life I couldn't have told which was Trumpeter. Of any difference between horses, except that of colour, I hadn't an idea. I scanned them all anxiously, and felt the ostler's eye upon me. This was unbearable. I pulled out my watch, glanced at it carelessly, and exclaimed—

"'By George, I'd no notion it was so early! H'm, on second thoughts, I won't start for a few minutes yet.'

"This was my only course—to wait until the other five owners of brown horses had driven home. I strolled back to the inn and talked and drank sherry, watching the crowd thin by degrees, and speeding the lingering mourners with all my prayers. The minutes dragged on till nothing short of a miracle could take me back in time to open the night-class. The widow drew near and talked to me. I answered her at random.

"Twice I revisited the stable, and the second time found but three horses left. I walked along behind them, murmuring, 'Trumpeter, Trumpeter!' in the forlorn hope that one of the three brutes would give a sign.

"'I beg your pardon, sir,' said the ostler; 'were you saying anything?'

"'No—nothing,' said I, and luckily he was called away at this moment to the further end of the stable. 'Oh,' sighed I, 'for Xanthus, horse of Achilles!'

"I felt inclined to follow and confide my difficulty to the ostler, but reflected that this wouldn't help me in the least: whereas, if I applied to a fellow-guest, he must (if indeed he could give the information) expose my previous hypocrisy to the ostler. After all, the company was dwindling fast. I went back and consumed more sherry and biscuits.

"By this six o'clock had gone, and no more than a dozen guests remained. One of these was my bovine friend, my neighbour at the funeral banquet, who now accosted me as I struggled with a biscuit.

"'So you've got over your hurry. Glad to find ye settlin' down so quick to our hearty ways.'

"He shook hands with the widow and sauntered out. Ten more minutes passed and now there were left only the widow herself and a trio of elderly men, all silent. As I hung about, trying to look unbounded sympathy at the group, it dawned upon me that they were beginning to eye me uneasily. I took a sponge cake and another glass of wine. One of the men—who wore a high stock and an edging of stiff grey hair around his bald head—advanced to me.

"'This funeral,' said he, 'is over.'

"'Yes, yes,' I stammered, and choked over a sip of sherry.

"'We are waiting—let me tap you on the back—'

"'Thank you.'

"'We are waiting to read the will.'

"I escaped from the room and rushed down to the stables. The ostler was harnessing the one brown horse that remained.

"I was thinking you wouldn't be long, sir. You're the very last, I believe, and here ends a long day's work.'

"I drove off. It was near seven by this, but I didn't even think of the night-class. I was wondering if the horse I drove were really Trumpeter. Somehow—whether because his feed of corn pricked him or no I can't say—he seemed a deal livelier than on the outward journey. I looked at him narrowly in the twilight, and began to feel sure it was another horse. In spite of the cool air a sweat broke out upon me.

"Farmer Retallack was up and dressed and leaning on a stick in the doorway as I turned into the yard.

"'I've been that worried about ye,' he began, 'I couldn't stay abed. Parson's been up twice from the schoolhouse to make inquiries. Where in the name o' goodness have 'ee been?'

"'That's a long story,' said I, and then, feigning to speak carelessly, though I heard my heart go thump—'How d'ye think Trumpeter looks after the journey?'

"'Oh, *he's* all right,' the old man replied indifferently; 'but come along in to supper.'

"Now, my dear sir"—the schoolmaster thus concluded his tale, tucking his umbrella tightly under his armpit, and tapping his right forefinger on the palm of his left hand—"these pagans whom I teach are as sensitive as I to ridicule. If I only knew how to take them—if only I could lay my finger on the weak spot—I'd send their whole fabric of silly superstitions tumbling like a house of cards."

This happened last Thursday week. Early this morning I crossed the road as usual with my thermometer, and found a strip of pink calico hanging from the brambles by the mouth of Scarlet's Well. I had seen the pattern before on a gown worn by one of the villager's wives, and knew the rag was a votive offering, hung there because her child, who has been ailing all the winter, is now strong enough to go out into the sunshine. As I bent the bramble carefully aside, before stooping over the water, Lizzie Polkinghorne came up the lane and halted behind me.

"Have 'ee heard the news?" she asked.

"No." I turned round, thermometer in hand.

"Why, Thomasine Slade's goin' to marry the schoolmaster! Their banns 'll be called first time nest Sunday."

We looked at each other, and she broke into a shout of laughter. Lizzie's laugh is irresistible.

II.—SILHOUETTES.

The small rotund gentleman who had danced and spun all the way to Gantick village from the extreme south of France, and had danced and smiled and blown his flageolet all day in Gantick Street without conciliating its population in the least, was disgusted. Towards dusk he crossed the stile which divides Sanctuary Lane from the churchyard, and pausing with a leg on either side of the rail, shook his fist back at the village which lay below, its grey roofs and red chimneys just distinguishable here and there between a foamy sea of apple-blossom and a haze of bluish smoke. He could not well shake its dust off his feet, for this was hardly separable on his boots from the dust of many other villages, and also it was mostly mud. But his gesture betokened extreme rancour.

"These Cor-rnishmen," he said, "are pigs all! There is not a Cor-rnishman that is not a big pig!"

He lifted the second leg wearily over the rail.

"As for Art—"

"Words failed him here, and he spat upon the ground, adding—

"Moreover, they shut up their churches!"

This was really a serious matter; for he had not a penny-piece in his pocket—the last had gone to buy a loaf—and there was no lodging to be had in the village. The month was April—a bad time to sleep in the open; and though the night drew in tranquilly upon a day of broad sunshine, the earth had by no means sucked down the late heavy rains. The church porch, however, had a broad bench on either side and faced the south, away from the prevailing wind. He had made a mental note of this early in the day, being schooled to anticipate such straits as the present. While, with a gait like a limping hare's, he passed up the narrow path between the graves, his eyes were busy.

The churchyard was narrow and surrounded by a high grey wall, mostly hidden by an inner belt of well-grown cypresses. On the south side the ranks of these trees were broken for some thirty feet, and here the back of a small dwelling-house abutted on the cemetery. There was one window only in the yellow-washed wall, and this window—a melancholy square framed in moss-stained plaster—looked straight into the church porch. The flageolet-player eyed it suspiciously; but the casement was shut and the blind drawn down. The whole aspect of the cottage proclaimed that its inhabitants were very poor folk—not at all the sort to tell tales upon a casual tramp if they spied him bivouacking upon holy ground.

He limped into the porch, and cast off the blue bag that was strapped upon his shoulders. Out of it he drew a sheep's-wool cape, worn very thin; and then turned the bag inside out, on the chance of a forgotten crust. The disappointment that followed he took calmly—being on the whole a sweet-tempered man, nor easily angered except by an affront on his vanity. His violent rancour against the people of Gantick arose from their indifference to his playing. Had they taken him seriously—had they even run out at their doors to listen and stare—he would not have minded their stinginess.

He who sleeps, sups. The little man passed the flat of his hand, in the dusk, over the two benches, chose the one which had fewest asperities of surface, tossed his bag and flageolet upon the other, pulled off his boots, folded his cape to make a pillow, and stretched himself at length. In less than ten minutes he was sleeping dreamlessly.

For four hours he slept without movement. But just above his head there hung a baize-covered board containing a list or two of the parish ratepayers and the usual notice of the spring training of the Royal Cornwall Eangers Militia. This last placard had broken from two of its fastenings, and towards midnight flapped loudly in an eddy of the light wind. The sleeper stirred, and passed a languid hand over his face. A spider within the porch had been busy while he slept, and his hand encountered gossamer.

His eyes opened. He sat upright, and lowered his bare feet upon the flags. Outside, the blue firmament was full of stars sparkling unevenly, as though the wind were trying in sport to puff them out. In the eaves of the porch he could hear the martins rustling in the crevices—they had returned but a few days back to their old quarters. But what drew the man to step out under the sky was the cottage-window over the wall.

The lattice was pushed back and the room inside was brightly lit. But between him and the lamp a white sheet had been stretched right across the window; and on this sheet two quick hands were weaving all kinds of clever shadows, shaping them, moving them, or reshaping them with the speed of summer lightning.

It was certainly a remarkable performance. The shadows took the forms of rabbits, swans, foxes, elephants, fairies, sailors with wooden legs, old women who smoked pipes, ballet-girls who pirouetted, anglers who bobbed for fish, twirling harlequins, and the profiles of eminent statesmen—all made with two hands and, at the most, the help of a tiny stick or piece of string. They danced and capered, grew large and then small, with such profusion of odd turns and changes that the flageolet-player began to giggle as he wondered. He remarked that the hands, whenever they were disentwined for a moment, appeared to be very small and plump.

In about ten minutes the display ceased, and the shadow of a woman's head and neck crossed the sheet, which was presently drawn back at one corner.

"Is that any better?" asked a woman's voice, low but distinct.

The flageolet-player started and bent his eyes lower, across the graves and into the shadow beneath the window. For the first time he was aware of a figure standing there, a little way out from the wall. As well as he could see, it was a young boy.

"Much better, mother. You can't think how you've improved at it this week."

"Any mistakes?"

"The harlequin and columbine seemed a little jerky. But your hands were tired, I know."

"Never mind that: they mustn't be tired and it's got to be perfect. We'll try them again."

She was about to drop the corner of the sheet when the listener sprang out towards the window, leaping with bare feet over the graves and waving his flageolet wildly.

"Ah, no—no, madame!" he cried. "Wait one moment, the littlest, and I shall inspire you."

"Whoever is that?" cried the woman's voice at the window.

The youth below faced round on the intruder. He was white in the face and had wanted to run, but mastered his voice and enquired gruffly—

"Who the devil are you?"

"I? I am an artist, and as such I salute madame and monsieur her son. She is greater artist than I, but I shall help her. They shall dance better this time, her harlequin and columbine. Why? Because they shall dance to my music—the music that I shall make here, on this spot, under the stars. *Tiens!* I shall play as if possessed. I feel that. I bet you. It is because I have found an artist—an artist in Gantick. O-my-good-lor! It makes me expand!"

He had pulled off his greasy hat, and stood bowing and smiling, showing his white teeth and holding up his flageolet, that the woman might see and be convinced.

"That's all very well," said the boy; "but my mother doesn't want it known that she practises at these shadows."

"Ha? It is perhaps forbidden by law?"

"Since you have found us out, sir," said the woman, "I will tell you why we are behaving like this, and trust you to tell nobody. I have been left a widow, in great poverty, and with this one son, who must be educated as well as his father was. Richard is a promising boy, and cannot be satisfied to stand lower in the world than his father stood. His father was an auctioneer. But we are left very poor—poor as mice: and how was I to get him better teaching than the Board Schools here? Well, six months ago, when sadly perplexed, I found out by chance that this small gift of mine might earn me a good income in London, at—at a music-hall—"

"Mother!" interjected the youth reprovingly.

"Pursue, madame," said the flageolet-player.

"Of course, sir, Richard doesn't like or approve of me performing at such places, but he agrees with me that it is necessary. So we are hiding it from everybody in the village, because we have always been respected here. We never guessed that anybody would see us from the churchyard, of all places, at this time of night. As soon as I have practised enough, we mean to travel up to London. Of course I shall change my name to something French or Italian, and hope nobody will discover—"

But the flageolet-player sat suddenly down upon a damp grave, and broke into hysterical laughter.

"Oh-oh-oh! Quick, madame! dance your pretty figures while yet I laugh and before I curse. O stars and planets, look down on this mad world, and help me play! And, O monsieur, your pardon if I laugh; for that either you or I are mad is a cock-sure. Dance, madame!"

He put the flageolet to his lips and blew. In a moment or two harlequin and columbine appeared on the screen, and began to caper nimbly, naturally, with the airiest graces. The tune was a jigging reel, and soon began to inspire the performer above. Her small dancers in a twinkling turned into a gambolling elephant, then to a pair of swallows. A moment after they were flower and butterfly, then a jigging donkey, then harlequin and columbine again. With each fantastic change the tune quickened and the dance grew wilder. At length, tired out, the woman spread her hands out wide against the sheet, as if imploring mercy.

The player tossed his flageolet over a headstone, and rolled back on the grave in a paroxysm of laughter. Above him the rooks had poured out of their nests, and were cawing in flustered circles.

"Monsieur," he gasped out, sitting up and wiping his eyes, "was it good this time?"

"Yes, it was."

"Then could you spare from the house one little crust of bread? For I am famished."

The youth went round the churchyard wall, and came back in a couple of minutes with some bread and cold bacon.

"Of course," said he, "if you should meet either of us in the village to-morrow, you will not recognise us."

The little man bowed. "I agree," said he, "with your mother, monsieur, that you must be educated at all costs."

THE DRAWN BLIND.

Silver trumpets sounded a flourish, and the javelin-men came pacing down Tregarrick Fore Street, with the sheriff's coach swinging behind them, its panels splendid with fresh blue paint and florid blazonry. Its wheels were picked out with yellow, and this scheme of colour extended to the coachman and the two lackeys, who held on at the back by leathern straps. Each wore a coat and breeches of electric blue, with a canary waistcoat, and was toned off with powder and flesh-coloured stockings at the extremities. Within the coach, and facing the horses, sat the two judges of the Crown Court and *Nisi Prius*, both in scarlet, with full wigs and little round patches of black plaister, like ventilators, on top; facing their lordships sat Sir Felix Felix-Williams, the sheriff, in a tightish uniform of the yeomanry with a great shako nodding on his knees, and a chaplain bolt upright by his side. Behind trooped a rabble of loafers and small boys, who shouted, "Who bleeds bran?" till the lackeys' calves itched with indignation.

I was standing in the archway of the Packhorse Inn, among the maids and stable-boys gathered to see the pageant pass on its way to hear the Assize sermon. And standing there, I was witness of a little incident that seemed to escape the rest.

At the moment when the trumpets rang out, a very old woman, in a blue camlet cloak, came hobbling out of a grocer's shop some twenty yards up the pavement, and tottered down ahead of the procession as fast as her decrepit legs would move. There was no occasion for hurrying to avoid the crowd; for the javelin-men had barely rounded the corner of the long street, and were taking the goosestep very seriously and deliberately. But she went by the Packhorse doorway as if swift horsemen were after her, clutching the camlet cloak across her bosom, glancing over her shoulder, and working her lips inaudibly. I could not help remarking the position of her right arm. She held it bent exactly as though she held an infant to her old breast, and shielded it while she ran.

54

A few paces beyond the inn-door she halted on the edge of the kerb, flung another look up the street, and darted across the roadway. There stood a little shop—a watchmaker's—just opposite, and next to the shop a small ope with one dingy window over it. She vanished up the passage, at the entrance of which I was still staring idly, when, half a minute later, a skinny trembling hand appeared at the window and drew down the blind.

I looked round at the men and maids; but their eyes were all for the pageant, now not a stone's-throw away.

"Who is that old woman?" I asked, touching Caleb, the head ostler, on the shoulder.

Caleb—a small bandy-legged man, with a chin full of furrows, and the furrows full of grey stubble—withdrew his gaze grudgingly from the sheriff's coach.

"What woman?"

"She that went by a moment since."

"She in the blue cloak, d'ee mean?—an old, ancient, wisht-lookin' body?"

"Yes."

"A timmersome woman, like?"

"That's it."

"Well, her name's Cordely Pinsent."

The procession reclaimed his attention. He received a passing wink from the charioteer, caught it on the volley and returned it with a solemn face; or rather, the wink seemed to rebound as from a blank wall. As the crowd closed in upon the circumstance of Justice, he turned to me again, spat, and went on—

"—Cordely Pinsent, widow of old Key Pinsent, that was tailor to all the grandees in the county so far back as I can mind. She's eighty-odd; eighty-five if a day. I can just mind Key Pinsent—a great, red, rory-cumtory chap, with a high stock and a wig like King George—'my royal patron' he called 'en, havin' by some means got leave to hoist the king's arms over his door. Such mighty portly manners, too—Oh, very spacious, I assure 'ee! Simme I can see the old Trojan now, with his white weskit bulgin' out across his doorway like a shop-front hung wi' jewels. Gout killed 'en. I went to his buryin'; such a stretch of experience does a young man get by time he reaches my age. God bless your heart alive, *I* can mind when they were hung for forgery!"

"Who were hung?"

"People," he answered vaguely; "and young Willie Pinsent."

"This woman's son?"

"Ay, her son—her ewe-lamb of a child. 'Tis very seldom brought up agen her now, poor soul! She's so very old that folks forgits about it. Do 'ee see her window yonder, over the ope?"

He was pointing across to the soiled white blind that still looked blankly over the street, its lower edge caught up at one corner by a dusty geranium.

"I saw her pull it down."

"Ah, you would if you was lookin' that way. I've a-seed her do 't a score o' times. Well, when the gout reached Key Pinsent's stomach and he went off like the snuff of a candle at the age of forty-two, she was left unprovided, with a son of thirteen to maintain or go 'pon the parish. She was a Menhennick, tho', from t'other side o' the Duchy—a very proud family—and didn't mean to dip the knee to nobody, and all the less because she'd demeaned hersel', to start with, by wedding a tailor. But Key Pinsent by all allowance was handsome as blazes, and well-informed up to a point that he read Shakespeare for the mere pleasure o't.

"Well, she sold up the stock-in-trade an' hired a couple o' rooms—the self-same rooms you see: and then she ate less 'n a mouse an' took in needle-work, plain an' fancy: for a lot o' the gentry's wives round the neighbourhood befriended her—though they had to be sly an' hide that they meant it for a favour, or she'd ha' snapped their heads off. An' all the while, she was teachin' her boy and tellin' 'en, whatever happened, to remember he was a gentleman, an' lovin' 'en with all the strength of a desolate woman.

"This Willie Pinsent was a comely boy, too: handsome as old Key, an' quick at his books. He'd a bold masterful way, bein' proud as ever his mother was, an' well knowin' there wasn' his match in Tregarrick for head-work. Such a beautiful hand he wrote! When he was barely turned sixteen they gave 'en a place in Gregory's Bank—Wilkins an' Gregory it was in those aged times. He still lived home wi' his mother, rentin' a room extra out of his earnin's, and turnin' one of the bedrooms into a parlour. That's the very room you're lookin' at. And when any father in Tregarrick had a bone to pick with his sons, he'd advise 'em to take example by young Pinsent—'so clever and good, too, there was no tellin' what he mightn't come to in time.'

"Well-a-well, to cut it short, the lad was too clever. It came out, after, that he'd took to bettin' his employers' money agen the rich men up at the Royal Exchange. An' the upshot was that one evenin', while he was drinkin' tea with his mother in his lovin' light-hearted way, in walks a brace o' constables, an' says, 'William Pinsent, young chap, I arrest thee upon a charge o' counterfeitin' old Gregory's handwritin', which is a hangin' matter!'

"An' now, sir, comes the cur'ous part o' the tale; for, if you'll believe me, this poor woman wouldn' listen to it—wouldn' hear a word o't. 'What! my son Willie,' she flames, hot as Lucifer—'my son Willie a forger! My boy, that I've missed, an' reared up, an' studied, markin' all his pretty takin' ways since he learn'd to crawl! Gentlemen,' she says, standin' up an' facin' 'em down, 'what mother knows her son, if not I? I give you my word it's all a mistake.'

"Ay, an' she would have it no other. While her son was waitin' his trial in jail, she walked the streets with her head high, scornin' the folk as she passed. Not a soul dared to speak pity; an' one afternoon, when old Gregory hissel' met her and began to mumble that 'he trusted,' an' 'he had little doubt,' an' 'nobody would be gladder than he if it proved to be a mistake,' she held her skirt aside an' went by with a look that turned 'en to dirt, as he said. 'Gad!' said he, 'she couldn' ha' looked at me worse if I'd been a tab!' meanin' to say 'instead o' the richest man in Tregarrick.'

56

"But her greatest freak was seen when th' Assizes came. Sir, she wouldn' even go to the trial. She disdained it. An' when, that mornin', the judges had driven by her window, same as they drove to-day, what d'ee think she did?

"She began to lay the cloth up in the parlour yonder, an' there set out the rarest meal, ready for her boy. There was meats, roasted chickens, an' a tongue, an' a great ham. There was cheese-cakes that she made after a little secret of her own; an' a bowl of junket, an inch deep in cream, that bein' his pet dish; an' all kind o' knick-knacks, wi' grapes an' peaches, an' apricots, an' decanters o' wine, white an' red. Ay, sir, there was even crackers for mother an' son to pull together, with scraps o' poetry inside. An' flowers—the table was bloomin' with flowers. For weeks she'd been plannin' it: an' all the forenoon she moved about an' around that table, givin' it a touch here an' a touch there, an' takin' a step back to see how beautiful it looked. An' then, as the day wore on, she pulled a chair over by the window, an' sat down, an' waited.

"In those days a capital trial was kept up till late into the night, if need were. By-an'-by she called up her little servin' gal that was then (she's a gran'mother now), an' sends her down to the court-house to learn how far the trial had got, an' run back with the news.

"Down runs Selina Mary, an' back with word—

"'They're a-summin'-up,' says she.

"Then Mrs. Pinsent went an' lit eight candles. Four she set 'pon the table, an' four 'pon the mantel-shelf. You could see the blaze out in the street, an' the room lit up, wi' the flowers, an' fruit, an' shinin' glasses—red and yellow dahlias the flowers were, that bein' the time o' year. An' over each candle she put a little red silk shade. You never saw a place look cosier. Then she went back an' waited: but in half-an-hour calls to Selina Mary agen:

"'Selina Mary, run you back to the courthouse, an' bring word how far they've got.'

"So the little slip of a maid ran back, and this time 'twas—

"'Missis, the judge has done; an' now they're considerin' about Master Willie.'

"So the poor woman sat a while longer, an' then she calls:

"'Selina Mary, run down agen, an' as he comes out, tell 'en to hurry. They must be finished by now.'

"The maid was gone twenty minutes this time. The evenin' was hot an' the window open; an' now all the town that wasn' listenin' to the trial was gathered in front, gazin' cur'ously at the woman inside. She was tittivatin' the table for the fiftieth time, an' touchin' up the flowers that had drooped a bit i' the bowls.

"But after twenty minutes Selina Mary came runnin' up the street, an' fetched her breath at the front door, and went upstairs slowly and 'pon tip-toe. Her face at the parlour door was white as paper; an' while she stood there the voices o' the crowd outside began to take all one tone, and beat into the room like the sound o' waves 'pon a beach.

"'Oh, missis—' she begins.

"'Have they finished?'

"The poor cheald was only able to nod.

"'Then, where's Willie? Why isn't he here?'

"'Oh, missis, they're goin' to hang 'en!'

"Mrs. Pinsent moved across the room, took her by the arm, led her downstairs, an' gave her a little push out into the street. Not a word did she say, but shut the door 'pon her, very gentle-like. Then she went back an' pulled the blind down slowly. The crowd outside watched her do it. Her manner was quite ord'nary. They stood there for a minute or so, an' behind the blind the eight candles went out, one by one. By the time the judges passed homeward 'twas all dark, only the blind showin' white by the street lamp opposite. From that year to this she has pulled it down whenever a judge drives by."

A GOLDEN WEDDING.

On the very spot which the railway station has usurped, with its long slate roof, wooden signal-box, and advertisements in blue and white enamel, I can recall a still pool shining between beds of the flowering rush; and to this day, as I wait for the train, the whir of a vanished water-wheel comes up the valley. Sometimes I have caught myself gazing along the curve of the narrow-gauge in full expectation to see a sagged and lichen-covered roof at the end of it. And sometimes, of late, it has occurred to me that there never was such a mill as I used to know down yonder; and that the miller, whose coat was always powdered so fragrantly, was but a white ghost, after all. The station-master and porters remember no such person.

But he was no ghost; for I have met him again this week, and upon the station platform. I had started at daybreak to fish up the stream that runs down the valley in curves roughly parallel to the railway embankment; and coming within sight of the station, a little before noon, I put up my tackle and strolled towards the booking-office. The water was much too fine for sport, and it seemed worth while to break off for a pipe and a look at the 12.26 train. Such are the simple pleasures of a country life.

I leant my rod against the wall, and was setting down my creel, when, glancing down the platform, I saw an old man seated on the furthest bench. Everybody knows how a passing event, or impression, sometimes appears but a vain echo of previous experience. Something in the lines of this old man's figure, as he leaned forward with both hands clasped upon his staff, gave me the sensation. "All this has happened before," I told myself. "He and I are playing over again some small and futile scene in our past lives. I wonder who he is, and what is the use of it?"

But there was something wanting in the picture to complete its resemblance to the scene for which I searched my memory.

The man had bent further forward, and was resting his chin on his hands and staring apathetically across the rails. Suddenly it dawned on me that there ought to be another figure on the bench—the figure of an old woman; and my memory ran back to the day after this railway was opened, when this man and his wife had sat together on the platform waiting to see the train come in—that fascinating monster whose advent had blotted out the very foundations of the old mill and driven its tenants to a strange home.

The mill had disappeared many months before that, but the white dust still hung in the creases of the miller's clothes. He wore his Sunday hat and the Sunday polish on his shoes; and his wife was arrayed in her best Paisley shawl. She carried also a bunch of cottage flowers, withering in her large hot hand. It was clear they had never seen a locomotive before, and wished to show it all respect. They had taken a smaller house in the next valley, where they attempted to live on their savings; and had been trying vainly and pitifully to struggle with all the little habits that had been their life for thirty-five years, and to adapt them to new quarters. Their faces were weary, but flushed with expectation. The man kept looking up the line, and declaring that he heard the rumble of the engine in the distance; and whenever he said this, his wife pulled the shawl more primly about her shoulders, straightened her back, and nervously re-arranged her posy.

When at length the whistle screamed out, at the head of the vale, I thought they were going to tumble off the bench. The woman went white to the lips, and stole her disengaged hand into her husband's.

"Startlin' at first, hey?" he said, bravely winning back his composure: "but 'tis wunnerful what control the driver has, they tell me. They only employ the cleverest men—"

A rattle and roar drowned the rest of his words, and he blinked and leant back, holding the woman's hand and tapping it softly as the engine rushed down with a blast of white vapour hissing under its fore wheels, and the carriages clanked upon each other, and the whole train came to a standstill before us.

The station-master and porter walked down the line of carriages, bawling out the name of the station. The driver leaned out over his rail, and the guard, standing by the door of his van, with a green flag under his arm, looked enquiringly at me and at the old couple on the bench. But I had only strolled up to have a look at the new train, and meant to resume my fishing as soon as it had passed. And the miller sat still, holding his wife's hand.

They were staring with all their eyes—not resentfully, though face to face with the enemy that had laid waste their habitation and swept all comfort out of their lives; but with a simple awe. Manifestly, too, they expected something more to happen. I saw the old woman searching the incurious features of the few passengers, and I thought her own features expressed some disappointment.

"This," observed the guard scornfully, pulling out his watch as he spoke, "is what you call traffic in these parts."

The station-master was abashed, and forced a deprecatory laugh. The guard—who was an up-country man—treated this laugh with contempt, and blew his whistle sharply. The driver answered, and the train moved on.

I was gazing after it when a woeful exclamation drew my attention back to the bench.

"Why, 'tis gone!"

"Gone?" echoed the miller's wife. "Of course 'tis gone; and of all the dilly-dallyin' men, I must say, John, you'm the dilly-dalliest. Why didn' you say we wanted to ride?"

"I thought, maybe, they'd have axed us. 'Twouldn' ha' been polite to thrust oursel's forrard if they didn' want our company. Besides, I thought they'd be here for a brave while—"

"You was always a man of excuses. You knew I'd set my heart 'pon this feat."

I had left them to patch up their little quarrel. But the scene stuck in my memory, and now, as I walked down the platform towards the single figure on the bench, I wondered, amusedly, if the woman had at length taken the ride alone, and if the procrastinating husband sat here to welcome her back.

As I drew near, I took note of his clothes for the first time. There was no white dust in the creases to-day. In fact, he wore the workhouse suit.

I sat down beside him, and asked if he remembered a certain small boy who had used to draw dace out of his mill-pond. With some difficulty he recalled my features, and by decrees let out the story of his life during the last ten years.

He and his wife had fought along in their new house, hiding their discomfort from each other, and abiding the slow degrees by which their dwelling should change into a home. But before that change was worked, the woman fell under a paralytic stroke, and their savings, on which they had just contrived to live, threatened to be swallowed up by the doctor's bill. After considering long, the miller wrote off to his only son, a mechanic in the Plymouth Dockyard, and explained the case. This son was a man of forty or thereabouts, was married, and had a long family. He could not afford to take the invalid into his house for nothing; but his daughters would look after their grandmother and she should have good medical care as well, if she came on a small allowance.

"So the only thing to be done, sir, was for my old woman to go."

"And you—?"

"Oh, I went into the 'House.' You see, there wasn' enough for both, livin' apart."

I stared down the line to the spot where the mill-wheel had hummed so pleasantly, and the compassionate sentence I was about to utter withered up and died on my lips.

"But to-day—Oh, to-day, sir—"

"What's happening to-day?"

"She's comin' down to see me for an hour or two; an' I've got a holiday to meet her. 'Tis our Golden Weddin', sir."

"But why are you meeting her at this station instead of Tregarrick? She can't walk, and you have no horse and trap; whereas there's always a 'bus at Tregarrick."

"Well, you see, sir, there's a very tidy little cottage below where they sell ginger-beer, an' I've got a whack o' vittles in the basket here, besides what William is bringin'—William an' his wife are comin' down with her. They'll take her back by the last train up; an' I thought, as 'twas so little a while, an' the benches here are so comfortable, we'd pass our day 'pon the platform here. 'Tis within sight o' the old home, too, or ruther o' the spot where the old home used to be: an' though 'tis little notice she seems to take o' things, one never can tell if poor creatures in that state *hain't* pleased behind all their dazed looks. What do you think, sir?"

The whistle sounded up the valley, and mercifully prevented my answer. I saw the woman for an instant as she was brought out of the train and carried to the bench. She did not recognise the man she had married fifty years before: but as we moved out of the station, he was sitting beside her, his face transfigured with a solemn joy.

SCHOOL FRIENDS.

"What ho, there!"

At this feudal summons I turned, and spied the Bashaw elbowing his way towards me through the Fleet Street crowd, his hat and tie askew and his big face a red beacon of goodwill. He fell on my neck, and we embraced.

"Is me recreant child returned? Is he tired at last av annihilatin' all that's made to a green thought in a green shade? An' did he homesickun by the Cornish Coast for the Street that Niver Sleeps, an' the whirroo an' stink av her, an' the *foomum et opase strepitumké*—to drink delight av battle with his peers, an' see the great Achilles whom he knew—meanin' meself?" The Bashaw's style in conversation, as in print, bristles with allusion.

I shook my head.

"I go back to-morrow, I hope. Business brought me up, and as soon as it's settled I pack."

"Too quick despairer—but I take it ye'll be bound just now for the Cheese. Right y'are; and I'll do meself the honour to lunch wid ye, at your expense."

Everyone knows and loves the Bashaw, *alias* the O'Driscoll, that genial failure. Generations of Fleet Street youths have taken advice and help from him: have prospered, grown reputable, rich, and even famous: and have left him where he stood. Nobody can remember the time when O'Driscoll was not; though, to judge from his appearance, he must have stepped upon the town from between the covers of an illustrated keepsake, such as our grandmothers loved— so closely he resembles the Corsair of that period, with his ripe cheeks, melting eyes, and black curls that twist like the young tendrils of a vine. The curls are dyed now-a-days, and his waist is not what it used to be in the picture-books; but time has worn nothing off his temper. He is perennially enthusiastic, and can still beat any journalist in London in describing a Lord Mayor's Show.

"You behould in me," he went on, with a large hand on my shoulder, "the victum av a recent eviction—a penniless outcast. 'Tis no beggar's petition that I'll be profferin', however, but a bargun. Give me a salad, a pint av hock, an' fill me pipe wid the Only Mixture, an' I'll repay ye across the board wid a narrative—the sort av God-forsaken, ord'nary thrifle that you youngsters turn into copy—may ye find forgiveness! 'Tis no use to me whatever. Ted O'Driscoll's instrument was iver the big drum, and he knows his limuts."

"Yes, me boy," he resumed, five minutes later, as he sat in the Cheshire Cheese, beneath Dr. Johnson's portrait, balancing a black-handled knife between his first and second fingers, and nodding good-fellowship to every journalist in the room, "the apartment in Bloomsbury is desolut; the furnichur'—what was lift av ut—disparsed; the leopard an' the lizard keep the courts where O'Driscoll gloried an' drank deep; an' the wild ass—meanin' by that the midical student on the fourth floor—stamps overhead, but cannot break his sleep. I've been evicted: that's the long and short av ut. Lord help me!—I'd have fared no worse in the ould country—here's to her! Think what immortal copy I'd have made out av the regrettable incident over there!" His voice broke, but not for self-pity. It always broke when he mentioned Ireland.

"Is it comfort ye'd be speakin'?" he began again, filling his glass. "Me dear fellow, divvle a doubt I'll fetch round tight an' safe. Ould Mick Sullivan—he that built the *Wild Girl*, the fastest vessel that iver put out av Limerick—ould Mick Sullivan used to swear he'd make any ship seaworthy that didn' leak worse than a five-barred gate. An' that's me, more or less. I'm an ould campaigner. But listen to this. Me feelin's have been wrung this day, and that sorely. I promised ye the story, an' I must out wid ut, whether or no."

It was the hour when the benches of the Cheese begin to empty. My work was over for the day, and I disposed myself to listen.

"The first half I spent at the acadimy where they flagellated the rudiments av polite learnin' into me small carcuss, I made a friend. He was the first I iver made, though not the last, glory be to God! But first friendship is like first love for the sweet taste it puts in the mouth. Niver but once in his life will a man's heart dance to that chune. 'Twas a small slip of a Saxon lad that it danced for then: a son av a cursed agint, that I should say it. But sorra a thought had I for the small boccawn's nationality nor for his own father's trade. I only knew the friendship in his pretty eyes an' the sweetness that knit our two sowls togither, like David's an' Jonathan's. Pretty it was to walk togither, an' discourse, an' get the strap togither for heaven knows what mischief, an' consowl each other for our broken skins. He'd a wonderful gift at his books, for which I reverenced um, and at the single-stick, for which I loved um. Niver to this day did I call up the ould play-ground widout behowldin' that one boy, though all the rest av the faces (the master's included) were vague as wather—wather in which that one pair av eyes was reflected.

"The school was a great four-square stone buildin' beside a windy road, and niver a tree in sight; but pastures where the grass would cut your boot, an' stone walls, an' brown hills around, like the rim av a saucer. All belonged to the estate that Jemmy Nichol's father managed—a bankrupt property, or next door to that. It's done better since he gave up the place; but when I've taken a glance at the landscape since (as I have, once or twice) I see no difference. To me 'tis the naked land I looked upon the last day av the summer half, when I said good-bye to Jemmy; for he was lavin' the school that same afternoon for Dublin, to cross over to England wid his father.

"Sick at heart was I, an' filled already wid the heavy sense of solitariness, as we stood by the great iron gate wishin' one another fare-ye-well.

"'Jemmy avick,' says I, 'dull, dull will it be widout ye here. And, Jemmy—send some av my heart back to me when ye write, as ye promise to do.'

"'Wheniver I lay me down, Ned,' he answered me (though by nature a close-hearted English boy), 'I'll think o' ye; an' wheniver I rise up I'll think o' ye. May the Lord do so to me, an' more also, if I cease from lovin' ye till my life's end.'

"So we kissed like a pair av girls, and off he was driven, leavin' a great hollow inside the rim av the hills. An' I ran up to the windy dormitory, stumblin' at ivery third step for the blindin' tears, and watched um from the window there growin' small along the road. 'Ye Mountains av Gilboa,' said I, shakin' my fist at the hills, 'let there be no dew, neither let there be rain upon ye;' for I hated the place now that Jemmy was gone.

"Well, 'twas the ould story—letters at first in plenty, then fewer, then none at all. Long before I came over to try my luck I'd lost all news of Jem: didn't know his address, even. Nor till to-day have I set eyes on um. He's bald-headed, me boy, and crooked-faytured, to-day; but I knew him for Jemmy in the first kick av surprise.

"I was evicted this mornin', as I've towld ye. Six years I've hung me hat up in those same apartments in Bloomsbury; and, till last year, aisy enough I found me landlord over a quarter's rent or two overjue. But last midsummer year the house changed hands; and bedad it began to be 'pay or quit.' This day it was 'quit.' The new landlord came up the stairs at the head av the ejectin' army: I got up from breakfast to open the door to um. I'd never set eyes on um since I'd been his tenant. Bedad, it was Jemmy!"

O'Driscoll paused, and poured himself another glass of hock.

"So I suppose," I said, "you ran into each other's arms, and kissed again with tears?"

"Then you suppose wrong," said he, and sat for a moment or two silent, fingering the stem of his glass. Then he added, more gently—

"I looked in the face av um, and said to meself, 'Jemmy doesn't remember me. If I introduce meself, I wonder what'll he do? Will he love me still, or will he turn me out?' An' by the Lord I didn't care to risk ut! I couldn't dare to lose that last illusion; an' so I put on me hat an' walked out, tellin' him nothing at all."

PARENTS AND CHILDREN.

I.—THE FAMILY BIBLE

There lived a young man at Tregarrick called Robert Haydon. His father was not a native of the town, but had settled there early in life and became the leading solicitor of the place. At the age of thirty-seven he married the daughter of a county magistrate, and by this step bettered his position considerably. By the time that Robert was born his parents' standing was very satisfactory. They were living well inside an income of £1,200 a year, had about £8,000 (consisting of Mrs. Haydon's dowry and Mr. Haydon's bachelor savings) safely invested, and were on visiting terms with several of the lesser county families.

In other respects they were just as fortunate. They had a sincere affection for each other, and coincident opinions on the proper conduct of life. They were people into whose heads a misgiving seldom or never penetrated. Their religious beliefs and the path of social duty stood as plain before them as their front gate and as narrow as the bridge which Mohammedans construct over hell. They loved Bob—who of four children was their only son—and firmly intended to do their best for him; and as they knew what was best for him, it followed that Bob must conform. He was a light-coloured, docile boy, with a pleasantly ingenuous face and an affectionate disposition; and he loved his parents, and learned to lean on them.

They sent him in time to Marlborough, where he wrote Latin verses of slightly unusual merit, and bowled with a break from the off which meant that there lay a thin vein of genius somewhere inside of him. When once collared, his bowling became futile; success made it deadly, and on one occasion in a school match against the M.C.C. he did things at Lord's which caused a thin gathering of spectators—the elderly men who never miss a match—to stare at him very attentively as he returned to the pavilion. They thought it worth while to ask, "Which 'Varsity was he bound for?"

Bob was bound for neither. He had to inherit, and consented to inherit, his father's practice without question. His consuming desire to go up to Oxford he hinted at once, and once only, in a conversation with his father; but Mr. Haydon "did not care to expose his son to the temptations which beset young men at the Universities"—this was the very text—and preferred to keep him under his own eye in the seclusion of Tregarrick.

To a young man who is being shielded from temptation in a small provincial town there usually happens one of two things. Either he takes to drink or to discreditable essays in love-making. It is to Bob's credit that he did neither; a certain delicate sanity in the fellow kept him from these methods of killing time. Instead, he spent his evenings at home; listened to his parents' talk; accepted their opinions on human conduct and affairs; and tumbled honourably into love with his sisters' governess.

Ethel Ormiston, the governess, was about a year older than Bob, good to look at, and the only being who understood what ailed Bob's soul during this time. She was in prison herself, poor woman. Mrs. Haydon asserted afterwards that Miss Ormiston had "deliberately set herself to inveigle" the boy; but herein Mrs. Haydon was mistaken. As a matter of fact Bob, having discovered someone obliging and intelligent enough to listen, dinned the story of his aspirations into the girl's ear with the persistent egoism of a hobbedehoy. It must be allowed, however, that the counsel she gave him would have annoyed his parents excessively.

"But I do sympathise with you," she said after listening to an immoderately long and peevish harangue; "and I should advise you to go to your father, as a first step, and ask to be paid a very small salary for the work you do—enough to set up in lodgings alone. At present you are pauperising yourself."

Bob did not quite understand—so she explained:

"You are twenty-one, and still receiving food and lodging from your parents as a dole. At your age, if a man receives anything at all from father or mother, he should be earning it as a right."

She spoke impatiently, and longed to add that he was also impoverishing his intellect. She felt a touch of contempt for him; but a touch of contempt may go with love, and, indeed, competent observers have held that this mixture makes the very finest cement. Certain it is that when Bob answered pathetically, "But I don't want to leave this roof, I—I *can't*, Miss Ormiston, you know!" she missed her opportunity of pointing out that this confession stultified every one of his previous utterances. She began a sentence, indeed, but broke off, with her grey eyes fixed on the ground; and when at length she lifted them, Bob felt something take him by the throat. The few words he proceeded to blurt out stunned him much as if a grenade had exploded close at hand. But when Miss Ormiston burst into tears and declared she must go upstairs at once and pack her box, he recovered, and, looking about, found the aspect of the world bewilderingly changed. There were valleys where hills had stood a moment before.

"I'll go at once and tell my father," he said, drawing a full breath and looking like the man he was for the moment.

"And," sobbed Miss Ormiston, "I'll go at once and pack my box."

Herein she showed foresight, for as soon as Bob's interview with his father was over, she was commanded to leave the premises in time to catch the early train next morning.

Then the Haydon family sat down and talked to Bob.

They began by pooh-poohing the affair. Then, inconsequently, they talked of disgrace, and of scratching his name out of the Family Bible, and said they would rather follow him to his grave than see him married to Miss Ormiston. Lastly, Mrs. Haydon asked Bob who had nursed him, and taught him to walk, and read and know virtue when he saw it. Bob, in the words of the poet, replied, "My mother." "Very well then," said Mrs. Haydon.

After forty-eight hours of this Bob wrote to Miss Ormiston, saying, "My father's indignation is natural, and can only be conquered by time. But I love you always."

Miss Ormiston replied, "Your father's indignation is natural, perhaps. But if you love me, it might be conquered by something else," or words to that effect. At any rate, her letter implied that as it was Bob, and not his father, who proposed to make her a wife, it was on Bob, and not on his father, that she laid the responsibility of fulfilling the promise.

But Bob was weak as water. Love had given him one brief glimpse of the real world: then his father and mother began to talk, and the covers of the Family Bible closed like gates upon his prospect. At the end of a week he wrote— "Nothing shall shake me, dear Ethel. Still, some consideration is due to them; for I am their only son."

To this Ethel Ormiston sent no answer; but reflected "And what consideration is due to me? for you are my only lover."

For a while Bob thought of enlisting, and then of earning an honest wage as a farm-labourer; but rejected both notions, because his training had not taught him that independence is better than respectability—yea, than much broadcloth. It was not that he hankered after the fleshpots, but that he had no conception of a world without fleshpots. In the end his father came to him and said—

"Will you give up this girl?"

And Bob answered—

"I'm sorry, father, but I can't."

"Very well. Rather than see this shame brought on the family, I will send you out to Australia. I have written to my friend Morris, at Ballawag, New South Wales, three hundred miles from Sydney, and he is ready to take you into his office. You have broken my heart and your mother's, and you must go."

And Bob—this man of twenty-one or more—obeyed his father in this, and went. I can almost forgive him, knowing how the filial habit blinds a man. But I cannot forgive the letter he wrote to Miss Ormiston—whom he wished to make his wife, please remember. Nevertheless she forgave him. She had found another situation, and was working on. Her parents were dead.

Five years passed, and Bob's mother died—twelve years, and his father died also, leaving him the lion's share of the money. During this time Bob had worked away at Ballawag and earned enough to set up as lawyer on his own account. But because a man cannot play fast and loose with the self-will that God gave him and afterwards expect to do much in the world, he was a moderately unsuccessful man still when the inheritance dropped in. It gave him a fair income for life. When the letter containing the news reached him, he left the office, walked back to his house, and began to think. Then he unlocked his safe and took out Ethel Ormiston's letters. They made no great heap; for of late their correspondence had dwindled to an annual exchange of good wishes at Christmas. She was still earning her livelihood as a governess.

Bob thought for a week, and then wrote. He asked Ethel Ormiston to come out and be his wife. You will observe that the old curse still lay on him. A man—even a poor one—that was worth kicking would have gone and fetched her; and Bob had plenty of money. But he asked her to come out and begged her to cable "Yes" or "No."

She cabled "Yes." She would start within the month from Plymouth, in the sailing-ship *Grimaldi*. She chose a sailing-ship because it was cheaper.

So Bob travelled down to Sydney to welcome his bride. He stepped on the *Grimaldi's* deck within five minutes of her arrival, and asked if a Miss Ormiston were on board. There advanced a middle-aged woman, gaunt, wrinkled and unlovely—not the woman he had chosen, but the woman he had made.

"Ethel?" was all he found to say.

"Yes, Bob; I am Ethel. And God forgive you."

Of the change in him she said nothing; but held out her hand with a smile.

"Marry me, Bob, or send me back: I give you leave to do either, and advise you to send me back. Twelve years ago you might have been proud of me, and so I might have helped you. As it is, I have travelled far, and am tired. I can never help you now."

And though he married her, she never did.

II.—BOANERGES.

"Bill Penberthy's come back, I hear."

The tin-smith was sharpening his pocket-knife on the parapet of the bridge, and, without troubling to lift his eyes, threw just enough interrogation into the remark to show that he meant it to lead to conversation. Every one of the dozen men around him held a knife, so that a stranger, crossing the bridge, might have suspected a popular rising in the village. But, as a matter of fact, they were merely waiting for their turn. There is in the parapet one stone upon which knives may be sharpened to an incomparable edge; and, for longer than I can remember, this has supplied the men of Gantick with the necessary excuse for putting their heads together on fine evenings and discussing the news.

"Ay, he's back."

"Losh, Uncle, I'd no idea you was there," said the tin-smith, wheeling round. "And how's your lad looking?"

"Tolerable—tolerable. 'A's got a black suit, my sonnies, and a white tie, and a soft hat that looks large on the head, but can be folded and stowed in your tail pocket." Complacency shone over the speaker's shrivelled cheeks, and beamed from his horn-spectacles. "You can tell 'en at a glance for a Circuit-man and no common Rounder."

"'A's fully knowledgeable by all accounts; learnt out, they tell me."

"You shall hear 'en for yourselves at meeting to-morrow. He conducts both services. Now don't tempt me any more, that's good souls: for when he'd no sooner set foot in th' house and kissed his mother than he had us all down on our knees giving hearty thanks in the most beautiful language, I said to myself, 'many's the time I've had two minds about the money spent in making ye a better man than your father;' but fare thee well, doubt! I don't begrudge it, an' there's an end."

A small girl came running down the street to the bridge-end.

"Uncle Penberthy," she panted, "your tall son—Mr. William—said I was to run down and fetch 'ee home at once."

"Nothin' wrong with 'en, I hope?"

"I think he's going to hold a prayer."

The little man looked at the blade of his knife for a moment, half regretfully: then briskly clasped it, slipped it into his pocket, and hobbled away after the messenger.

The whitewashed front of the Meeting House was bathed, next evening, with soft sunset yellow when Mr. Penberthy the elder stole down the stairs between the exhortations, as his custom was, and stood bareheaded in the doorway respiring the cool air. As a deacon he temperately used the privileges of his office, and one of these was a seat next the door. The Meeting House was really no more than a room—a long upper chamber over a store; and its stairway descended into the street so sharply that it was possible, even for a short-armed man, to sit on the lowest step and shake hands with a friend in the street.

The roadway was deserted for a while. Across the atmosphere there reigned that hush which people wonder at on Sundays, forgetting that nature is always still and that nine-tenths of the week's hubbub is made by man. Down the pale sky came a swallow, with another in chase: their wings were motionless as they swept past the doorway, but the air whizzed with the speed of their flight, and in a moment was silent again. Then from the upper room a man's voice began to roar out upon the stillness. It roared, it broke out in thick sobs that shook the closed windows in their fastenings, it wrestled with emotion for utterance, and, overcoming it, rose into a bellow again; but, whether soaring or depressed, the strain upon it was never relaxed. Uncle Penberthy, listening to his son, felt an oppression of his own chest and drew his breath uneasily.

The tin-smith came round the corner and halted by the door.

"That son o' yours is a boundless man," he observed with an upward nod.

"How did he strike ye this morning?"

"I don't remember to have been so powerfully moved in my life. Perhaps you and me being cronies for thirty year, and he your very son, may have helped to the more effectual working; but be that as it may, I couldn't master my dinner afterwards, and that's the trewth. Ah, he's a man, Uncle; and there's no denying we wanted one of that sort to awaken us to a fit sense. What a dido he do kick up, to be sure!"

The tin-smith shifted his footing uneasily as if he had something to add.

"I hope you won't think it onneighbourly or disrespectful that I didn' come agen this evenin'," he begun, after a pause.

"Not at all, Jem, not at all."

"Because, you see—"

"Yes, yes, I quite see."

"I wouldn' have ye think—but there, I'm powerful glad you see." His face cleared. "Good evenin' to ye, Uncle!"

He went on with a brisker step, while Uncle Penberthy drew a few more lingering breaths and climbed the stairs again to the close air of the meeting-room.

"I'm afraid, father, that something in my second exhortation displeased you," said the Rev. William Penberthy as he walked home from service between his parents. He was a tall fellow with a hatchet-shaped face and eyes set rather closely together.

"Not at all, my son. What makes ye deem it?" The little man tilted back his bronzed top-hat and looked up nervously.

"Because you went out in the middle of service."

"'Tis but father's habit, William," old Mrs. Penberthy made haste to explain, laying a hand on his arm. She was somewhat stouter of build and louder of voice than her husband, but stood in just the same awe of her son. "He's done it regular since he was appointed deacon."

"Why?" asked William, stonily.

Uncle Penberthy pulled off his hat to extract a red handkerchief from its crown, removed his spectacles, and wiped them hurriedly.

"Them varmints of boys," he stammered, "be so troublesome round the door—occasion'lly, that is."

"Was that so to-night?"

"Why, no."

"But you were absent at least twenty minutes—all through the silent prayer and half way through the third exhortation." He gazed sternly at the amiable old man. "You didn't hear me treat that difficulty in Colossians, two, twenty to twenty-three? If you have time, we'll discuss it after private worship to-night. If I can make you see it in what I am sure is the right light, it will lead you to think more seriously of that glass of beer you have fallen into the habit of taking with your supper."

It is but a fortnight since the Rev. William Penberthy came home; but in that fortnight his father and mother have aged ten years. The old man, when I took him my watch to regulate the other day—for on week-days he is a watch-maker—began to ask questions, as eagerly as a child, about the village news. It turned out that, for a whole week, he had not been down to sharpen his knife upon the bridge. He has given up his glass of beer, too, and altogether the zeal of his house is eating him up.

This morning the new minister climbed into the van with his carpet-bag. He is off to some Conference or other, and will be back again the day after to-morrow. Ten minutes after he had gone his father and mother shut up the shop and went out together. They mean to take a whole holiday and hear all the news. It was pitiful to see their fumbling haste as they helped one another to put up the shutters; and almost more pitiful to mark, as they hurried down the street arm in arm, their conscientious but feeble endeavour to look something more staid than a couple of children just out of school.

TWO MONUMENTS.

MY DEAR YOUNG LADY,—

Our postman here does not deliver parcels until the afternoon—which nobody grumbles at, because of his infirmity and his long and useful career. The manuscript, therefore, of your novel, *Sunshine and Shadow*, has not yet reached me. But your letter—in which, you beg me to send an opinion upon the work, with some advice upon your chances of success in literature—I found on my breakfast-table, as well as the photograph which you desire (perhaps wisely) to face the title-page. I trust you will forgive the slight stain in the lower left-hand corner of the portrait, which I return: for it is the strawberry-season here, and in course of my reflections I had the misfortune to let the cardboard slip between my fingers and fall across the edge of the plate.

I have taken the resolution to send my advice before it can be shaken by a perusal of *Sunshine and Shadow*. But it is difficult nevertheless. I might say bluntly that, unless the camera lies, your face is not one to stake against Fame over a game of hazard. You remember John Lyly's "Cupid and my Campaspe"?—and how Cupid losing,

"*down he throws*
The coral of his lip, the rose
Growing on's cheek (but none lenows how) ..."

—and so on, with the rest of his charms, one by one? I might assure you that when maidens play against Fame they risk all these treasures and more, without hope of leniency from their opponent, who (you will note) is the same sex. But you will answer by return of post, that this is no business of mine, and that I exhibit the usual impertinence of man when asked to consider woman's serious aspiration. You will protest that you are ready to stake all this. Very well, then: listen, if you have patience, to a little story that I came upon, a week since, about a man who spent his days at this game of hazard. It was called *The Two Monuments*.

When the Headmaster of the Grammar-School came to add up the marks for the term's work and examination—which he always did without a mistake—it was discovered that in the Upper Fourth (the top form) Thompson had beaten Jenkins *major* by sixteen. So Thompson received a copy of the *Memoirs of Eminent Etonians*, bound in tree-calf, and took it home under his arm, wondering what "Etonians" were, but too proud to ask. And Jenkins *major* received nothing; and being too weak to punch Thompson's head (as he desired) waylaid him opposite the cemetery gate on his way home, and said—

"*Parvenu!*"

—which was doubly insulting; for, in the first place, French was Thompson's weakest subject, and secondly, his father was a haberdasher in a small way, who spoke with awe of the Jenkinses as a family that had practised law in the town for six generations. Thompson himself was aware of the glamour such a lineage conferred. It was wholly due to his ignorance of French that he retorted—

"You're another!"

Young Jenkins explained the term, with a wave of his hand towards the cemetery gate.

"You'll find my family in there, and inside a rail of their own. And you needn't think I wanted that prize. *I*'ve got a grandfather."

So, no doubt, had Thompson; but, to find him, he must have consulted the parish books and searched among the graves at the northern end of the burial-ground for one decorated with a tin label and the number 2054. He gazed in at the sacred acre of the Jenkinses and the monuments emblazoned with "J.P.," "Recorder of this Borough," "Clerk of the Peace for the County," and other proud appendices in gilt lettering: and, in the heat of his heart, turned upon Jenkins *major*.

"You just wait till we die, and see which of us two has the finer tombstone!"

Thereupon he stalked home and read the *Memoirs of Eminent Etonians*, and learnt from their perusal that it was indeed possible to earn a finer tombstone than any Jenkins possessed. At the end of the Christmas term, too, he acquired a

70

copy of Dr. Smiles's famous work on *Self-Help*, and this really set his feet in the path to his desire.

He determined, after weighing the matter carefully, to be a poet: for it seemed to him that of all the noble professions this was the only one the initial expense of which could be covered by his patrimony. The paper, ink, and pens came cheaply enough (though the waste was excessive); and for his outfit of high thoughts and emotions he pawned not merely the possessions that you, my dear young lady, are so willing to cast on the table—charms of face and graces of person—for, as a man, he valued these lightly; but the strength in his arms, the taste of meat and wine, the cunning of horsemanship, of boat-sailing, of mountain-climbing, the breathless joy of the diver, the languid joy of the dancer, the feel of the canoe-paddle shaken in the rapid, the delicious lassitude of sleep in wayside-inns, and lastly the ecstasy of love and fatherhood—all these he relinquished for a tombstone that should be handsomer than Jenkins's. Jenkins, meanwhile, was articled to his father, and, having passed the necessary examinations with credit, became a solicitor and married into a county family.

Thompson, I need hardly tell you, was by this time settled in London and naturally spent a good deal of his leisure time in Westminster Abbey. The monuments there profoundly affected his imagination, and gave him quite new ambitions with regard to the tombstone that towered at the back of all his day-dreams. When first he trod the Embankment, in thin boots with a few pence in his pocket, it had appeared to him in slate with a terrific inscription in gilt letters—inscriptions in which "Benefactor of His Species," "Take him for All in All We shall not Look upon his Like Again" took the place of the pettifogging "Clerk of the Peace" or "J.P." tagged on to the names of the Jenkinses. By degrees, however, he abated a little of the inscription and made up for it by trebling the costliness of the stone.

From slate it grew to granite—to marble—to alabaster, with painted cherubs and a coat of arms. At one time he brooded, for a whole week, over a flamboyant design with bosses of lapis lazuli at the four corners; and only gave it up for a life-size recumbent figure in alabaster with four gryphons supporting the sarcophagus. As the soles of his boots thickened with prosperity, so did his stone grow in solidity. Finally an epic of his—*Adrastus*—took the town by storm, and three editions were exhausted in a single week. When this happened, he sat down with a gigantic sheet of cartridge paper before him and spent a whole year in setting out the elaborated design. By his will he left all his money to pay for the structure: for his father and mother were dead and he had neither wife nor child.

When all was finished he rubbed his hands, packed up his bag and took a third-class ticket down to his native town, to have a contemptuous look at the Jenkins monuments and see how Jenkins *major* was getting on.

Jenkins *major* was up in the cemetery, among his fathers. And on top of Jenkins rested a granite cross—sufficiently handsome, to be sure, for a solicitor, but nothing out of the way. "J.P." was carved upon it; though, as Jenkins had an absurdly long Christian name (Marmaduke Augustus St. John), these letters were squeezed a bit in the right arm of the cross. Underneath was engraved—

71

"_ERECTED BY HIS DISCONSOLATE WIFE AND CHILDREN.

  A Father kind, a Husband dear,
 A faithful Friend, lies buried here_."

Thompson perused the doggerel once, twice, and a third time; and chuckled contemptuously. "So Jenkins has come to this. God bless me, how life in a provincial town does narrow a man!"

"*A Father kind, a Husband dear...*"

—and he went away chuckling, but with no malice at all in his breast.

Jenkins slept forgiven beneath his twopenny-halfpenny tombstone, and Thompson, reflecting that not only was his own monument designed (with a canopy of Carrara marble), but the cost of it invested in the three per cents., walked contentedly back to the station, repeating on his way with gentle scorn—

  "*A Father kind, a Husband dear, A faithful Friend, lies buried here.*"

The jingle lulled him asleep in his railway carriage, and he awoke in London. Driving home, he paid the cabby, rushed up to his room three stairs at a bound, unlocked his safe and pulled out the great design. In one corner he had even drawn up a list of the eminent men who should be his pall-bearers. Certainly such a tomb would make Jenkins turn in his grave.

He spread the plan on the table, with a paper-weight on each corner, and sat down before it. After considering it for an hour, he arose dissatisfied.

"Jenkins had a heap of flowers over him—common flowers, to be sure, but fresh enough. I dare say I could arrange for a supply, though. It's that confounded doggerel—

'*A Father kind, a Husband dear.*'

"That's Mrs. Jenkins's taste, I suppose. Still—of course I could better the verse; but one can't stick up a lie over one's remains. I wish to God I had a disconsolate wife, or a child, if only to spite Jenkins."

And I believe, my dear young lady, that underneath his tomb (whereon there now stands a marble figure of Fame and blows a gilt trumpet) he is still wishing it.

EGG-STEALING.

It wanted less than an hour to high water when Miss Marty Lear heard her brother's boat take ground on the narrow beach below the garden, and set the knives and glasses straight while she listened for the click of the garden-latch.

A line of stunted hazels ran along the foot of the garden and hid the landing-place from Miss Lear as she stood at the kitchen window gazing down steep alleys of scarlet runners. But above the hazels she could look across to the fruit-growing village of St. Kits, and catch a glimpse at high tide of the intervening river, or towards low water of the mud-banks shining in the sun.

It was Miss Lear's custom to look much on this landscape from this window: had, in fact, been her habit for close upon forty years. And this evening, when the latch clicked at length, and her brother in his market-suit come slouching up the path between the parallels of garden-stuff, her eyes rested all the while upon the line of grey water above and beyond his respectable hat.

Nor, when he entered the kitchen, hitched this hat upon a peg in the wall—where its brim accurately fitted a sort of dull halo in the whitewash—did he appear to want any welcome from her. He was a long-jawed man of sixty-five, she a long-jawed woman of sixty-one; and they understood each other's ways, having kept this small and desolate farm together for thirty years—that is, since their father's death.

A cold turnip-pasty stood on the table, with the cider-jug that Job Lear regularly emptied at supper. These suggested no small-talk, and the pair sat down to eat in silence.

It was only while holding out his plate for a second helping of the pasty that Job spoke with a full mouth.

"Who d'ee reckon I ran across to-day, down in Troy?"

Miss Marty cut the slice without troubling to say that she had not a notion.

"Why, that fellow Amos Trudgeon," he went on.

"Yes?"

"'Pears to me you must be failin' if you disremembers 'en: son of old Sal Trudgeon, that used to keep the jumble-shop 'cross the water: him that stole our eggs back-along, when father was livin'."

"I remember."

"I thought you must. Why, you gave evidence, to be sure. Be dashed! now I come to mind, if you wasn' the first to wake the house an' say you heard a man hollerin' out down 'pon the mud."

"Iss, I was."

"An' saved his life, though you did get 'en two months in Bodmin Gaol by it. Up to the arm-pits he was, an' not five minutes to live, when we hauled 'en out, an' wonderin' what he could be doin' there, found he'd been stealin' our eggs. He inquired after you to-day."

"Did he?"

"Iss. 'How's Miss Marty?' says he. 'Agein' rapidly,' says I. The nerve that some folks have! Comes up to me as cool as my lord and holds out a hand. He've a-grown into a sort of commercial; stomach like a bow-window, with a watch-guard looped across. I'd a mind to say 'Eggs' to 'en, it so annoyed me."

"I hope you didn't."

"No. 'Twould have seemed like bearin' malice. 'Tis an old tale, after all, that feat of his."

"Nine an' thirty year, come seventeenth o' September next. Did he say any more?"

"Said the weather-glass was risin', but too fast to put faith in."

"I mean, did he ask any more about me?"

"Iss: wanted to know if you was married. I reckon he meant that for a bit o' pleasantness."

"Not that! Ah, not that!"

Job laid down knife and fork with their points resting on the rim of his plate, and, with a lump of pasty in one cheek, looked at his sister. She had pushed back her chair a bit, and her fingers were plucking the edge of the table-cloth.

"Not that!" she repeated once more, and hardly above a whisper. She did not lift her eyes. Before Job could speak—

"He was my lover," she said, and shivered.

"Mar—ty—"

She looked up now, hardened her ugly, twitching face, forced her eyes to meet her brother's, and went on breathlessly—

"I swear to you, Job—here, across this table—he was my lover; and I ruined 'en. He was the only man, 'cept you and father, that ever kissed me; and I betrayed 'en. As the Lord liveth, I stood up in the box and swore away his name to save mine. An' what's more, he made me."

"Mar—ty Lear!"

"Don't hinder me, Job. It's God's truth I'm tellin' 'ee. His folks were a low lot, an' father'd have broken every bone o' me. But we used to meet in the orchard 'most every night. Don't look so, brother. I'm past sixty, an' nothin' known; an' now evil an' good's the same to me."

"Go on."

"Well, the last night he came over 'twas spring tides, an' past the flood. I was waitin' for 'en in the orchard, down in the corner by the Adam's Pearmain. We could see the white front o' the house from there, and us in the dark shadow: and there was the gap handy, that Amos could snip through at a pinch—you fenced it up yoursel' the very summer that father died in the fall. That night, Amos was late an' the dew heavy, an' no doubt I lost my temper waitin' out there in the long grass. We had words, I know; an' I reckon the tide ran far out while we quarrelled. Anyway, he left me in wrath, an' I stood there under the appletree, longin' for 'en to come back an' make friends again. But the time went on, an' I didn' hear his footstep—no, nor his oars pullin' away—though hearkenin' with all my ears.

"An' then I heard a terrible sound." Miss Marty paused and drew the back of her hand across her dry lips before proceeding.

"—a terrible sound—a sort of low breathin', but fierce; an' something worse, a suck-suckin' of the mud below; an' I ran down. I suppose, in his anger, he took no care how he walked round the point (for he al'ays moored his boat round the point, out o' sight), an' went wide an' was taken. There he was, above his knees in it, and far out it seemed to me, in the light o' the young moon. For all his fightin', he heard me, and whispers out o' the dark—

"'Little girl, it's got me. Hush! don't shout, or they'll catch you.'

"'Can't you get out?' I whispered back.

"'No,' says he, 'I'm afraid I can't, unless you run up to the linhay an' fetch a rope.'

"It was no more I stayed to hear, but ran up hot-foot to the linhay and back inside the minute, with the waggon rope.

"'Hold the end,' he panted, 'and throw with all your strength.' And I threw, but the rope fell short. Twice again I threw, but missed each cast by a yard and more. He wouldn't let me come near the mud.

"Then I fell to runnin' to an' fro on the edge o' the firm ground, an' sobbin' between my teeth because I could devise nothin'. And all the while he was fightin' hard.

"'I'll run an' call father an' Job,' says I.

"'Hush'ee now! Be you crazed? Do you want to let 'em know all?'

"'But it'll kill you, dear, won't it?'

"'Likely it will,' said he. Then, after a while of battlin', he whispers again, 'Little girl, I don't want to die. Death is a cold end. But I reckon you shall save me an' your name as well. Take the rope, coil it as you run, and hang it back in the linhay, quick! Then run you to the hen-house an' bring me all the eggs you can find. Be quick and ax no questions, for it's little longer I can hold up. It's above my waist,' he says.

"I didn' know what he meant, but ran for my life to the linhay, and hung up the rope, an' then to the hen-house. I could tell prety well where to find a dozen eggs or more in the dark, an' in three minutes I'd groped about an' gathered 'em in the lap o' my dress. Then back I ran. I could just spy 'en—a dark spot out there in the mud.

"'How many?' he axed, an' his voice was like a rook's.

"'A dozen, or near.'

"'Toss 'em here. Don't come too nigh, an' shy careful, so's I can catch.'

"I stepped down pretty nigh to the brim o' the mud an' tossed 'em out to him. Three fell short in my hurry, but the rest he got hold of somehow.

"'That's right,' he calls, hoarse and low, 'they'll think egg-stealin' nateral to a low family like our'n. Now back to your room—undress—an' cry out, sayin', there's a man shoutin' for help down 'pon the mud; and, dear, be quick! When you wave your candle twice at the window, I'll shout like a Trojan.'

"An' I did it, Job; for the cruelty in a fearful woman passes knowledge. An' you rescued 'en an' he went to gaol. For he said 'twas the only way. An' his mother took it as quite reasonable that her husband's son should take to the bad—'twas the way of all them Trudgeons. Father to son, they was of no account. Egg-stealin' was just the little hole-an'-corner wickedness that 'd come nateral to 'em."

"I rec'lect now," said Job Lear very slowly, "that the wain-rope was wet i' my hands when I unhitched 'en that night from the hook, an' I wondered, it bein' the end of a week's dryth. But in the dark an' the confusion o' savin' the wastrel's life it slipped my thoughts, else—"

"Else you'd ha' wetted it wi' the blood o' my back, Job. But the rope's been frayed to powder this many year. An' you needn't look at me like that. I'm past sixty, an' I've done my share of repentin'. He didn't say if he was married, did he?"

SEVEN-AN'-SIX.

The old fish-market at Troy was just a sagged lean-to roof on the northern side of the Town Quay, resting against the dead wall of the harbour-master's house, and propped in front by four squat granite columns. This roof often let in rain enough to fill the pits worn in the paving-stones by the feet of gossiping generations; and the whole was wisely demolished a few years back to make place for a Working Men's Institute—a red building, where they take in all the chief London newspapers. Nevertheless I have, in some moods, caught myself hankering after the old shelter, where the talk was unchartered always, and where no notices were suspended against smoking; and I know it used to be worth visiting on dirty evenings about the time of the Equinox, when the town-folk assembled to watch the high tide and the chances of its flooding the streets about the quay.

Early one September afternoon, about two years before its destruction, a small group of watermen, a woman or two, and a fringe of small children were gathered in the fish-market around a painter and his easel. The painter—locally known as Seven-an'-Six—was a white-haired little man, with a clean-shaven face, a complexion of cream and roses, a high unwrinkled brow, and blue eyes that beamed an engaging trustfulness on his fellow-creatures, of whom he stood ready to paint any number at seven shillings and sixpence a head. As this method of earning a livelihood did not allow him to sojourn long in one place— which, indeed, was far from his desire—he spent a great part of his time upon the cheaper seats of obscure country vehicles. He delighted in this life of perennial transience, and enjoyed painting the portraits which justified it; and was, on the whole, one of the happiest of men.

Just now he was enjoying himself amazingly, being keenly alive not merely to the crowd's admiration, but to the rare charm of that which he was trying to paint. Some six paces before him there leant against one of the granite pillars a woman of exceeding beauty: her figure tall, supple, full of strength, in every line, her face brown and broad-browed, with a heavy chin that gave character to the rest of her features, and large eyes, black as sloes, that regarded the artist and the group at his elbow with a sombre disdain. The afternoon sunshine slanted down the pillar, was broken by the mass of dark hair she rested against it, and ran down again along her firm and rounded arm to the sun-bonnet she dangled by its strings. Behind her, the quay's edge shone bright against the green water of the harbour, where, half a cable's length from shore, a small three-masted schooner lay at anchor, with her Blue Peter fluttering at the fore.

"He's gettin' her to-rights," observed one of the crowd.

A woman said, "I wish I'd a-been took in my young days, when I was comely."

"Then, whyever wasn't 'ee, Mrs. Slade?"

"Well-a-well, my dear, I'm sure I dunno. Three ha'af-crowns is a lot o' money to see piled in your palm, an' say 'Fare thee well; increase!' Store 's no sore, as my old mother used to say."

"But," argued a man, "when once you've made up your mind to the gallant speckilation, you never regret it—danged if you do!"

"Then why hasn't 'ee been took, Thomas, in all these years?"

"Because that little emmet o' doubt gets the better o' me every time. 'Tis like holdin' back from the Fifteen Balls: you feel sure in your own mind you'll be better wi'out the drink, but for your life you durstn't risk the disapp'intment. Over this matter I'll grant ye that I preaches what I can't practise. But my preachin' is sound. Therefore, I bid ye all follow the example o' Cap'n Hosken here, who, bein' possessed wi' true love for 'Liza Saunders, is havin' her portrait took for to hang up in his narrow cabin out to sea, an' remind hissel' o' the charms that bide at home a-languishin'."

"That's not my reason, though," said Captain Hosken, a sunburnt and serious man, at the painter's elbow.

"Then what may it be, makin' so bold?"

"I'll tell ye when the painting's done."

"A couple of strokes, and it's finished," said the artist, cocking his head on one side and screwing up his blue eyes. "There, I'll tell you plainly, friend, that my skill is but a seven-and-sixpenny matter, or a trifle beyond. It does well enough what it pretends to do; but this is a subject I never ought to have touched. I know my limits. You'll see, sir," he went on, in a more business-like tone, "I've indicated your ship here in the middle distance. I thought it would give the portrait just that touch of sentiment you would desire."

The faces gathered closer to stare. 'Liza left the pillar, stretched herself to her full height, and came forward, tying the strings of her sun-bonnet.

"'Tis the very daps of her!" was Captain Hosken's comment as he pulled out his three half-crowns. "As for the *Rare Plant*, what you've put in might be took for a vessel; and if a man took it for a vessel, he might go on to take it for a schooner; but I'd be tolerable sorry if he took it for a schooner o' which I was master. Hows'ever, you've put in all 'Liza's good looks an' enticingness. 'Tis a picture I'm glad to own, an' be dashed to the sentiment you talked about!"

He took the portrait carefully from the easel, and held it before him, between his open palms.

"Neighbours all," he began, his rather stupid face overspread with an expression of satisfied cunning, "I promised to tell 'ee my reasons for havin' 'Liza's portrait took. They're rather out o' the common, an' 'Liza hersel' don't guess what they be, no more than the biggest fool here present amongst us."

He looked from the man Thomas, from whose countenance this last innuendo glanced off as from a stone wall, to 'Liza, who answered him with a puzzled scowl. Her foot began to tap the paving-stone impatiently.

"When I gazes 'pon 'Liza," he pursued, "my eyes be fairly dazzled wi' the looks o' her. I allow that. She's got that build, an' them lines about the neck an' waist, an' them red-ripe lips, that I feels no care to look 'pon any other woman. That's why I took up wi' her, an' offered her my true heart. But strike me if I'd counted 'pon her temper; an' she's got the temper of Old Nick! Why, only last evenin'—the very evenin' before I sailed, mark ye—she slapped my ear. She did, though! Says I, down under my breath, 'Right you are my lady! we'll be quits for

77

that.' But, you see, I couldn' bear to break it off wi' her, because I didn' want to miss her beautiful looks."

The women began to titter, and 'Liza's face to flame, but her lover proceeded with great complacency:

"Well, I was beset in my mind till an hour agone, when—as I walked down here with 'Liza, half mad to take leave of her, and sail for Rio Grande, and likewise sick of her temper—I sees this gentleman a-doin' pictures at seven-an'-six; and thinks I, 'If I can get 'en to make a copy of 'Liza's good looks, then I shall take off to sea as much as I want of her, an' the rest, temper included, can bide at home till I calls for it. That's all I've got to say. 'Liza's a beauty beyond compare, an' her beauty I worships, an' means to worship. But if any young man wants to take her, I tell him he's welcome. So long t' ye all!"

Still holding the canvas carefully a foot from his waistcoat, to avoid smearing it, he sauntered off to the quay-steps, and hailed his boat to carry him aboard the *Rare Plant*. As he passed the girl he had thus publicly jilted, her fingers contracted for a second like a hawk's talons; but she stood still, and watched him from under her brows as he descended the steps. Then with a look that, as it travelled in a semi-circle, obliterated the sympathy which most of the men put into their faces, and the sneaking delight which all the women wore on theirs, she strode out of the fish-market and up the street.

Seven-an'-Six squeezed the paint out of his brushes, packed up his easel and japanned box, wished the company good-day, and strolled back to his inn. He was sincerely distressed, and regretted a hundred times in the course of that evening that he had parted with the portrait and received its price before Captain Hosken had made that speech. He would (he told himself) have run his knife through the canvas, and gladly forfeited the money. As it was, he lingered long over the supper it procured, and ate heartily.

A mile beyond the town, next morning, Boutigo's van, in which he was the only passenger, pulled up in front of a roadside cottage. A bundle and a tin box were hoisted up by Boutigo, and a girl climbed in. It was 'Liza.

"Oh, good morning!" stammered the little painter.

"I'm going to stay with my aunt in Truro, and seek service," the girl announced, keeping her eye upon him, and her colour down with an effort. "Where are you bound?"

"I? Oh, I travel about, now in one place, next day in another—always moving. It's the breath of life to me, moving around."

"That must be nice! I often wonder why men tie themselves up to a wife when they might be free to move about like you, and see the world. What does a man want to tack a wife on to him when he can always carry her image about?" She laughed, without much bitterness.

"But—" began the amiable painter, and checked himself. He had been about to confess that he himself owned a wife and four healthy children. He saw this family about once in two months, and it existed by letting out lodgings in a small unpaintable town. He was sincerely fond of his wife, who made every allowance for his mercurial nature; but it suddenly struck him that her portrait hung in the parlour at home, and had never accompanied him on his travels.

He was silent for a minute or two, and then began to converse on ordinary topics.

THE REGENT'S WAGER.

Boutigo's van—officially styled *The Vivid*—had just issued from the Packhorse Yard, Tregarrick, a leisurely three-quarters of an hour behind its advertised time, and was scaling the acclivity of St. Fimbar's Street in a series of short tacks. Now and then it halted to take up a passenger or a parcel; and on these occasions Boutigo produced a couple of big stones from his hip-pockets and slipped them under the hind-wheels, while we, his patrons within the van, tilted at an angle of 15° upon cushions of American cloth, sought for new centres of gravity, and earnestly desired the summit.

It was on the summit, where the considerate Boutigo gave us a minute's pause to rearrange ourselves and our belongings, that we slipped into easy and general talk. An old countryman, with an empty poultry-basket on his knees, and a battered top-hat on the back of his head, gave us the cue.

"When Boutigo's father had the accident—that was back in 'fifty-six,' and it broke his leg an' two ribs—the van started from close 'pon the knap o' the hill here, and scat itself to bits against the bridge at the foot just two and a half minutes after."

I suggested that this was not very fast for a runaway horse.

"I dessay not," he answered; "but 'twas pretty spry for a van slippin' *backwards*, and the old mare diggin' her toes in all the way to hold it up."

One or two of the passengers grinned at my expense, and the old man pursued—

"But if you want to know how fast a hoss *can* get down St. Fimbar's hill, I reckon you've lost your chance by not axin' Dan'l Best, that died up to the 'Sylum twelve years since; though, poor soul, he'd but one answer for every question from his seven-an'-twentieth year to his end, an' that was 'One, two, three, four, five, sis, seven.'"

"Ah, the poor body! his was a wisht case," a woman observed from the corner furthest from the door.

"Ay, Selina, and fast forgotten, like all the doin's and sufferin's of the men of old time." He reached a hand round his basket, and touching me on the knee, pointed back on Tregarrick. "There's a wall," he said, and I saw by the direction of his finger that he meant the wall of the county prison, "and beneath that wall's a road, and across that road's a dismal pool, and beyond that pool's a green hillside, with a road athurt it that comes down and crosses by the pool's head. Standin' 'pon that hillside you can see a door in the wall, twenty feet above the ground, an' openin' on nothing. Leastways, you could see it once; an' even now, if ye've good eyesight, ye can see where they've bricked it up."

I could, in fact, even at our distance, detect the patch of recent stone-work; and knew something of its history.

"Now," the old man continued, "turn your looks to the right and mark the face of Tregarrick town-clock. You see it, hey?"—and I had time to read the hour on its dial before Boutigo jolted us over the ridge and out of sight of it—"Well, carry them two things in your mind: for they mazed Dan'l Best an' murdered his brother Hughie."

And, much as I shall repeat it, he told me this tale, pausing now and again to be corroborated by the woman in the corner. The history, my dear reader, is accurate enough—for Boutigo's van.

There lived a young man in Tregarrick in the time of the French War. His name was Dan'l Best, and he had an only brother Hughie, just three years younger than himself. Their father and mother had died of the small-pox and left them, when quite young children, upon the parish: but old Walters of the Packhorse—he was great-grandfather of the Walters that keeps it now—took a liking to them and employed them, first about his stables and in course of time as post-boys. Very good post-boys they were, too, till Hughie took to drinking and wenching and cards and other devil's tricks. Dan'l was always a steady sort: walked with a nice young woman that was under-housemaid up to the old Lord Bellarmine's at Castle Cannick, and was saving up to be married, when Hughie robbed the mail.

Hughie robbed the mail out of doubt. He did it up by Tippet's Barrow, just beyond the cross-roads where the scarlet gig used to meet the coach and take the mails for Castle Cannick and beyond to Tolquite. Billy Phillips, that drove the gig, was found in the ditch with his mouth gagged, and swore to Hughie's being the man. The Lord Chief Justice, too, summed up dead against him, and the jury didn't even leave the box. And the moral was, "Hughie Best, you're to be taken to the place whence you come from, ancetera, and may the Lord have mercy upon your soul!"

You may fancy what a blow this was to Dan'l; for though fine and vexed with Hughie's evil courses, he'd never guessed the worst, nor anything like it. Not a doubt had he, nor could have, that Hughie was guilty; but he went straight from the court to his young woman and said, "I've saved money for us to be married on. There's little chance that I can win Hughie a reprieve; and, whether or no, it will eat up all, or nearly all, my savings. Only he's my one brother. Shall I go?" And she said, "Go, my dear, if I wait ten years for you." So he borrowed a horse for a stage or two, and then hired, and so got to London, on a fool's chase, as it seemed.

The fellow's purpose, of course, was to see King George. But King George, as it happened, was daft just then; and George his son reigned in his stead, being called the Prince Regent. Weary days did Dan'l air his heels with one Minister of the Crown after another before he could get to see this same Regent, and 'tis to be supposed that the great city, being new to him, weighed heavy on his spirits. And all the time he had but one plea, that his brother was no more than a boy and hadn't an ounce of vice in his nature—which was well enough beknown to all in Tregarrick, but didn't go down with His Majesty's advisers: while as for the Prince Regent, Dan'l couldn't get to see him till the Wednesday evening that

Hughie was to be hanged on the Friday, and then his Royal Highness spoke him neither soft nor hopeful.

"The case was clear as God's daylight," said he: "the Lord Chief Justice tells me that the jury didn't even quit the box."

"Your Royal Highness must excuse me," said Dan'l, "but I never shall be able to respect that judge. My opinion of a judge is, he should be like a stickler and see fair play; but this here chap took sides against Hughie from the first. If I was you," he said, "I wouldn't trust him with a Petty Sessions."

"Well, you may think how likely this kind of speech was to please the Prince Regent. And I've heard that Dan'l; was in the very article of being pitched out, neck and crop, when he heard a regular caprouse start up in the antechamber behind him, and a lord-in-waiting, or whatever he's called, comes in and speaks a word very low to the Prince.

"Show him in at once," says he, dropping poor Dan'l's petition upon the table beside him; and in there walks a young officer with his boots soiled with riding and the sea-salt in his hair, like as if he'd just come off a ship; and hands the Prince a big letter. The Prince hardly cast his eye over what was written before he outs with a lusty hurrah, as well he might, for this was the first news of the taking of St. Sebastian.

"Here's news," said he, "to fill the country with bonfires this night."

"Begging your Royal Highness's pardon," answers the officer, pulling out his watch; "but the mail coaches have left St. Martin's Lane"—that's where they started from, as I've heard tell—"these twenty minutes."

"Damn it!" says Dan'l Best and the Prince Regent, both in one breath.

"Hulloa! Be you here still?" says the Prince, turning sharp round at the sound of Dan'l's voice. "And what be you waiting for?"

"For my brother Hughie's reprieve," says Dan'l.

"Well, but 'tis too late now, anyway," says the Prince.

"I'll bet 'tis not," says Dan'l, "if you'll look slippy and make out the paper."

"You can't do it. 'Tis over two hundred and fifty miles, and you can't travel ten miles an hour all the way like the coach."

"It'll reach Tregarrick to-morrow night," says Dan'l, "an' they won't hang Hughie till seven in the morning. So I've an hour or two to spare, and being a post-boy myself, I know the ropes."

"Well," says his Royal Highness, "I'm in a very good temper because of this here glorious storming of St. Sebastian. So I'll wager your brother's life you don't get there in time to stop the execution."

"Done with you, O King!" says Dan'l, and the reprieve was made out, quick as lightning.

Well, sir, Dan'l knew the ropes, as he said; and moreover, I reckon there was a kind of freemasonry among post-boys; and the two together, taken with his knowledge o' horseflesh, helped him down the road as never a man was helped before or since. 'Twas striking nine at night when he started out of London with the reprieve in his pocket, and by half-past five in the morning he spied

Salisbury spire lifting out of the morning light. There was some hitch here—the first he met—in getting a relay; but by six he was off again, and passed through Exeter early in the afternoon. Down came a heavy rain as the evening drew in, and before he reached Okehampton the roads were like a bog. Here it was that the anguish began, and of course to Dan'l, who found himself for the first time in his life sitting in the chaise instead of in the saddle, 'twas the deuce's own torment to hold himself still, feel the time slipping away, and not be riding and getting every ounce out of the beasts: though, even to *his* eye, the rider in front was no fool. But at Launceston soon after daybreak he met with a misfortune indeed. A lot of folks had driven down overnight to Tregarrick to witness the day's sad doings, and there wasn't a chaise to be had in the town for love or money.

"What do I want with a chaise?" said Dan'l, for of course he was in his own country now, and everybody knew him. "For the love of God, give me a horse that'll take me into Tregarrick before seven and save Hughie's life! Man, I've got a reprieve!"

"Dear lad, is that so?" said the landlord, who had come down, and was standing by the hotel door in nightcap and bedgown. "I thought, maybe, you was hurrying to see the last of your brother. Well, there's but one horse left in stable, and that's the grey your master sold me two months back; and he's a screw, as you must know. But here's the stable key. Run and take him out yourself, and God go with 'ee!"

None knew better than Dan'l that the grey was a screw. But he ran down to the stable, fetched the beast out, and didn't even wait to shift his halter for a bridle, but caught up the half of a broken mop-handle that lay by the stable door, and with no better riding whip galloped off bare-back towards Tregarrick.

Aye, sir, and he almost won his race in spite of all. The hands o' the town clock were close upon seven as he came galloping over the knap of the hill and saw the booths below him and sweet-stalls and standings—for on such days 'twas as good as a fair in Tregarrick—and the crowd under the prison wall. And there, above them, he could see the little open doorway in the wall, and one or two black figures there, and the beam. Just as he saw this the clock struck its first note, and Dan'l, still riding like a madman, let out a scream, and waved the paper over his head; but the distance was too great. Seven times the clapper struck, and with each stroke Dan'l screamed, still riding and keeping his eyes upon that little doorway. But a second or two after the last stroke he dropped his arm suddenly as if a bullet had gone through it, and screamed no more. Less than a minute after, sir, he pulled up by the bridge on the skirt of the crowd, and looked round him with a silly smile.

"Neighbours," says he, "I've a-got great news for ye. We've a-taken St. Sebastian, and by all acounts the Frenchies'll be drove out of Spain in less'n a week."

There was silence in Boutigo's van for a full minute; and then the old woman spoke from the corner:

"Well, go on, Sam, and tell the finish to the company."

"Is there more to tell?" I asked.

"Yes, sir," said Sam, leaning forward again, and tapping my knee very gently, "there were *two men* condemned at Tregarrick, that Assize; and two men put to death that morning. The first to go was a sheep-stealer. Ten minutes after, Dan'l saw Hughie his brother led forth; and stood there and watched, with the reprieve in his hand. His wits were gone, and he chit-chattered all the time about St. Sebastian."

LOVE OF NAOMI.

I.

The house known as Vellan's Rents stands in the Chy-pons over the waterside, a stone's throw beyond the ferry and the archway where the toll-keeper used to live. You may know it by its exceeding dilapidation and by the clouds of steam that issue on the street from one of its windows. The sill of this window stands a bare foot above the causeway, and glancing down into the room as you pass, you will see the shoulders of a woman stooping over a wash-tub. When first I used to pass this window the woman was called Naomi Bricknell; later it was Sarah Ann Polgrain; and now it is (euphemistically) Pretty Alice. One goes and makes way for another, but the wash-tub is always there and the rheumatic fever; and while these remain they will never lack, as they have never lacked yet, for a woman to do battle for dear life between them.

But my story concerns the first of these only, Naomi Bricknell. She and her mother occupied two rooms in Vellan's Rents as far back as I can remember, and were twisted with the fever about once in every six months. For this they paid one shilling a week rent. If you lift the latch and push the front door open, you seem at first to be looking down a well; for a flight of thirty-two steps plunges straight from the threshold to the quay door and a square of green water there. And when the sun is on the water at the bottom of this funnel, the effect is pretty. But taking note of the cold wind that rushes up this stairway and into the steaming room where the wash-tub stands, you will understand how it comes that each new tenant takes over the rheumatic fever as one of the fixtures.

In a room to the right of the stairway, and facing Naomi's, lived a middle-aged man who was always known as Long Oliver. This man was a native of the port, and it was understood that he and Naomi had been well acquainted, years ago, before he started on his first voyage and some time before Naomi married. Tiring of the sea in time, he had found work on the jetties and rented this room for sixpence a week. In these days he and Naomi rarely spoke to each other beyond exchanging a "Good-morning" when they met on the stairway, nor did he show any friendliness beyond tapping at her mother's door and inquiring about her once a day whenever she happened to be down with the fever. I have made researches and find that the rest of the house was tenanted at that time by a working block-maker, with his wife and four children; a widow and her son just returned from sea with an injured spine; a young couple without children. But these do not come into the tale.

Now the history of Naomi was this. She was married at three-and-twenty to Abe Bricknell, a young sailor of the port, and as steady as a woman could wish.

In the third year of their married life, and a week after obtaining his certificate, he sailed out of Troy as mate of a fruit-ship, a barque, that never came back, nor was sighted again after passing the Lizard lights.

Naomi—a tall up-standing woman with deep, gentle eyes, like a cow's, and a firm mouth that seldom spoke—took her affliction oddly. She neither wailed nor put on mourning. She looked upon it as a matter between herself and her Maker, and said:

"God has done this thing to me; therefore I have finished with Him. I am no man to go and revenge myself by breaking all the Commandments. But I am a woman and can suffer. Let Him do His worst: I defy Him."

So she never set foot inside church again, nor offered any worship. The week long she worked as a laundress, and sat through the Sundays with her arms folded, gloomily fighting her duel. When the fever wrenched her arms and lips as she stood by the wash-tub, she set her teeth and said, "I can stand it. I can match all this with contempt. He can kill, but that's not beating me."

Her mother, a large and pale-faced woman of sixty, with an apparently thoughtful contraction of the lips, in reality due to a habit of carrying pins in her mouth, watched Naomi anxiously during this period of her life. And Long Oliver watched her too, though secretly, with eyes screwed up after the fashion of men who have followed the sea.

One day he stopped her on the stairs and asked, abruptly:

"When be you thinkin' to marry again?"

"Never," she answered, straight and at once, halting with a hand on her hip and eyeing him.

"Dear me; but you will, I hope."

"Not to you, anyway."

"Laws me, no! I don't want 'ee; haven't wanted 'ee these ten years. But I'd a reason for askin'."

"Then I'm sure I don't know what it can be."

"True—true. Look'ee here, my dear; 'tis ordained for you to marry agen."

"Aw? Who by?"

"Providence."

Naomi had treated Long Oliver badly in days gone by, but could still talk to him with more freedom than to other men. Still standing with a hand on her hip, she let fall a horrible sentence about the Almighty—all the more horrible in that it came deliberately, without emphasis, and from quiet lips.

"Woman!" cried a voice above them.

They turned, looked up, and saw the bent figure of a man framed in the street doorway. This was William Geake, who walked in from Gantick every Saturday to collect the sixpences and shillings of Vellan's Rents for its landlord, a well-to-do wine and spirit merchant at Tregarrick. As a man of indisputable probity and an unwearying walker, Geake was entrusted with many odd jobs of this kind in the country round, filling in with them such idle corners as his trade of carpenter and undertaker to Gantick village might leave in the six working days. On

Sundays he put on a long black coat, and became a Rounder, or Methodist local-preacher, walking sometimes twenty miles there and back to terrify the inhabitants of outlying hamlets about their future state.

"Woman!" cried William Geake, "Down 'pon your knees an' pray God the roof don't fall on 'ee for your vile words."

"I reckon," retorted Naomi quietly, with a glance up at the worm-riddled rafters, "you'd do more good by speakin' to the landlord."

William Geake had a high brow and bright, nervous eyes, betokening enthusiasm; but he had also a long and square jaw that meant stubbornness. This jaw now began to protrude and his lips to straighten.

"Down 'pon your knees!" he repeated.

Naomi turned her eyes from him to Long Oliver, who leant against the staircase wall with his arms crossed and a veiled amusement in his face. With a slightly heightened colour, but no flutter of the voice, she repeated her blasphemy; and then, pulling a shilling from her worn purse, tendered it to Geake. This, of course, meant "Mind your own business"; but he waved her hand aside.

"Down 'pon your knees, woman!" he shouted thunderously. Then, as she showed no disposition to obey, he added, grimly, "Eh? but somebody shall intercede for thee afore thou'rt a minute older."

And pulling off his hat there and then, he knelt down on the doorstep, with the soles of his hob-nailed boots showing to the street.

"Get up, an' don't make yoursel' a may-game," said Naomi hurriedly, as one or two children stopped their play, and drew around to stare.

"Father in heaven," began William Geake, in a voice that fetched the women-folk, all up and down the Chy-pons, to their doors, "Thou, whose property is ever to have mercy, forgive this blaspheming woman! Suffer one who is Thy servant, though a grievous sinner, to intercede for her afore she commits the sin that cannot be forgiven; to pluck her as a brand from the burning—"

By this, the women and a loafing man or two had clustered round, and Colliver's coal-cart had rattled up and come to a standstill. The Chy-pons is the narrowest street in Troy, and Colliver's driver could hardly pass now, except over William Geake's legs.

"Draw in your feet, brother Geake," he called out, "or else pray short."

One or two women giggled at this. But Geake did not seem to hear. For five good minutes he prayed vociferously, as was his custom in meeting-house; then rose, replaced his hat, dusted his knees, held out his hand for Naomi's shilling, and wrote her the customary voucher in his most business-like manner, and without another word. But there was a triumphant look in his eyes that dared Naomi to repeat her offence, and she very nearly wept as she felt that the words would not come. This and the shame of publicity drove her back into her room as Geake passed down the stairs to collect the other rents. A few women still hung about the doorway as he emerged, some twenty minutes later. But he marched down Chy-pons with head erect and eyes fixed straight ahead.

II.

On the following Saturday, when Geake called, Naomi was standing at her wash-tub. She had seen him pass the window, and, hurriedly wiping her hands, and pulling out her shilling, placed it ostentatiously in the very centre of the deal table by the door; then had just time to plunge her hands in the soap-suds again before he knocked. Try as she would, she could not keep back a blush at the remembrance of last week's scene, and half looked for him to make some allusion to it.

His extremely business-like air reassured her. She nodded towards the shilling without removing her hands from the tub. He took it, including in a polite good-morning both Naomi and her mother, who was huddled in an arm-chair before the fire and recovering from an attack of the fever, wrote out his voucher solemnly, set it in the exact spot where the shilling had stood, took up his hat, hesitated for less than a second, replaced his hat on the table, and, pulling a chair towards him, dropped on his knees, and began to pray aloud.

The old woman by the fire slewed her head painfully round and stared at him, then at Naomi. But Naomi was standing with her back to them both, and her hands soaping the linen in the tub—gently, however, and without any splashing. She therefore let her head sink back on the cushion, and assumed that peculiarly dejected air, commonly reserved by her for the consolations of religion.

On this occasion William Geake prayed in a low and level tone, and very briefly. He made no allusion to last Saturday, but put up an earnest petition for blessings upon "our two sisters here," and that they might learn to accept their appointed portion with resignation, yea, even with a holy joy. At the end of two minutes he rose, and was about to dust his knees, after his usual custom, but, becoming suddenly aware of the difference in cleanliness between Naomi's lime-ash and the floors of the various meeting-houses of his acquaintance, refrained. This little piece of delicacy did not escape Naomi, though her shoulders were still bent over the tub, to all seeming as resolutely as ever.

"Well, I swow that was very friendly of Mister Geake!" the old woman ejaculated, as the door closed behind him. "'Tisn't everybody'd ha' thought what a comfort a little scrap o' religion can be to an old woman in my state."

"He took a great liberty," said Naomi snappishly.

"Well, he might ha' said as much as 'By your leave,' to be sure; an' now you say so, 'twas makin' a bit free to talk about our dependence—an' in my own kitchen too."

"He meant our dependence on th' Almighty," Naomi corrected, still more snappishly. "William Geake's an odd-fangled man, but you might give 'en credit for good-feelin'. An', what's more, though I don't hold wi' Christian talk, if a man have a got beliefs, I respect 'en for standin' to 'em without shame."

"But I thought, a moment ago—" her mother began, and then subsided. She was accustomed to small tangles in her own processes of thought, and quite incapable, after years of blind acceptance, of correcting Naomi's logic.

No more was said on the matter. The next Saturday, after receiving his shilling, Mr. Geake knelt down without any hesitation. It was clear he wished this prayer to be a weekly institution, and an institution it became.

The women never knelt. Naomi, indeed, had never sanctioned the innovation, unless by her silence, and her mother assisted only with a very lugubrious "Amen," being too weak to stir from her chair. As the months passed, it became evident to Geake that her strength would never come back. The fever had left her, apparently for good; but the rheumatism remained, and closed slowly upon the heart. The machine was worn out.

When the end came, Naomi had been doing the work single-handed for close upon twelve months. She could always get a plenty of work, and now took in a deal too much for her strength, to settle the doctor's and undertaker's bills, and buy herself a black gown, cape, and bonnet. The funeral, of course, took place on a Sunday. Geake, on the Saturday afternoon, knocked gently at Naomi's door. His single intent was to speak a word or two of sympathy, if she would listen. Remembering her constant attitude under the Divine scourge, he felt a trifle nervous.

But there lay the shilling in the centre of the table, and there stood Naomi in a cloud of steam, hard at work on an immoderate pile of washing—even a man's miscalculating eye could see that it was immoderate.

"I didn't call—" he began, with a glance towards the shilling.

"No; I know you didn't. But you may so well take it all the same."

Geake had rehearsed a small speech, but found himself making out and signing the voucher as usual; and, as usual, when it was signed, he drew over a chair, and dropped on his knees. In prayer-meeting he was a great hand at "improving" an occasion of bereavement; but here again his will to speak impressively suddenly failed him. His words were:

"Lord, there were two women grinding at a mill; the one was taken, and t'other left. She that you took, you've a-carr'd beyond our prayers; but O, be gentle, be gentle, to her that's left!"

He arose, and looked shyly, almost shamefacedly, at Naomi. She had not turned. But her head was bowed; and, drawing near, he saw that the scalding tears were falling fast into the wash-tub. She had not wept when her husband was lost, nor since.

"Go away!" she commanded, before he could speak, turning her shoulders resolutely towards him.

He took up his hat, and went out softly, closing the door softly behind him.

His eye, which was growing quick to read Naomi's face, saw at once, as he entered the room a week later, that she deprecated even the slightest reference to her weakness. It also told him—he had not guessed it before—that her emotional breakdown had probably more to do with physical exhaustion than with any eloquence of his. The pile of washing had grown, and the woman's face was grey with fatigue.

Geake, as he made out the voucher, cast about for a polite mode of hinting that this kind of thing must not go on. Nevertheless it was Naomi who began.

"Look here," she said, as he put down the voucher; "there ain't goin' to be no more prayin', eh?"

"Why, to be sure there is," he answered with a show of great cheerfulness; and reached for a chair.

"I'd liefer you didn't. I don't want it. I don't hold by any o't. You'm very kind," she went on, her voice trembling for an instant and then recovering its firmness, "and I reckon it soothed mother. But I reckon it don't soothe me. I reckon it rubs me the wrong way. There's times, when I hears a body prayin', that I wishes we was Papists again and worshipped images, that I might throw stones at 'em!"

She paused, looked up into Geake's devouring eyes, and added, with a poor attempt at a laugh:

"So you see, I'm wicked, an' don't want to be saved."

Then the man broke forth:

"Saved? No, I reckon you don't! Wicked? Iss, I reckon you be! But saved you shall be—ay, if you was twice so wicked. Who'll do it? I'll do it—I alone. I don't want your help. I want to do it in spite of 'ee: an' I'll lay that I do! Be your wickedness deep as hell, an' I'll reach down a hand to the roots and pluck it up: be your salvation stubborn as Death, I'll wrestle wi' the Lord for it. If I sell my own soul for't, yours shall be redeemed!"

He slammed down his fist on the rickety deal table, which promptly collapsed flat on the floor, with its four legs splayed under the circular cover.

"Bein' a carpenter—" Geake began to stammer apologetically, and in a totally different tone.

For a second—two seconds—the issue hung between tears and laughter. An hysterical merriment twinkled in Naomi's eyes.

But the strength of Geake's passion saved the situation. He stepped up to Naomi, laid a hand on each shoulder, and shook her gently to and fro.

"Listen to me! As I hold 'ee now, so I take your fate in my hands. Naomi Bricknell, you've got to be my wife, so make up your mind to that."

She cowered a little under his grasp; put out a hand to push him off; drew it back; and broke into helpless sobbing. But this time she did not command him to go away.

Fifteen minutes later William Geake left Vellan's Rents with joy on his face and a broken table under his arm.

And two days later Naomi's face wore a look of demure happiness when Long Oliver stopped her on the staircase and asked,

"Is it true, what I hear?"

"It is true," she answered.

"An' when be the banns called?"

"There ain't goin' to be no banns."

"Hey?"

"There ain't goin' to be no banns; leastways, there ain't goin' to be none called. We'm goin' to the Registry Office. You look all struck of a heap. Was you hopin' to be best man?"

"Well, I reckoned I'd take a hand in the responses," he answered; and seemed about to say more, but turned on his heel and went back to his room, shutting the door behind him.

III.

We pass to a Saturday morning, two years later, and to William Geake's cottage at the western end of Gantick village.

Naomi had plucked three fowls and trussed them, and wrapping each in a white napkin, had packed them in her basket with a dozen and a half of eggs, a few pats of butter, and a nosegay or two of garden-flowers—Sweet Williams, marigolds, and heart's-ease: for it was market-day at Tregarrick. Then she put on boots and shawl, tied her bonnet, and slung a second pair of boots across her arm: for the roads were heavy and she would leave the muddy pair with a friend who lived at the entrance of the town, not choosing to appear untidy as she walked up the Fore Street. These arrangements made, she went to seek her husband, who was busy planing a coffin-lid in the workshop behind the cottage, and ruminating upon to-morrow's sermon.

"You'll be about startin'," he said, lifting his head and pushing his spectacles up over his eye-brows.

Naomi set her basket down on his work-table, and drew her breath back between her teeth—which is the Cornish mode of saying "Yes." "I want you to make me a couple of skivers," she said. "Aun' Hambly sent over word she'd a brace o' chicken for me to sell, an' I was to call for 'em: an' I'd be ashamed to sell a fowl the way she skivers it."

William set down his plane, picked up an odd scrap of wood and cut out the skewers with his pocket-knife; while Naomi watched with a smile on her face. Whether or no William had recovered her soul, as he promised, she had certainly given her heart into his keeping. The love of such a widow, he found, is as the surrender of a maid, with wisdom added.

The skewers finished, he walked out through the house with her and down the garden-path, carrying the basket as far as the gate. The scent of pine-shavings came with him. Half-way down the path Naomi turned aside and picking a sprig of Boy's Love, held it up for him to smell. The action was trivial, but as he took the sprig they both laughed, looking in each other's eyes. Then they kissed; and the staid woman went her way down the road, while the staid man loitered for a moment by the gate and watched her as she went.

Now as he took his eyes away and glanced for an instant in the other direction, he was aware of a man who had just come round the angle of the garden hedge and, standing in the middle of the road, not a dozen yards off, was also staring after his wife.

This stranger was a broad-shouldered fellow in a suit of blue seaman's cloth, the trousers of which were tucked inside a pair of Wellington boots. His complexion was brown as a nut, and he wore rings in his ears: but the features were British enough. A perplexed, ingratiating and rather silly smile overspread them.

The two men regarded each other for a bit, and then the stranger drew nearer.

"I do believe that was Na'mi," he said, nodding his head after the woman's figure, that had not yet passed out of sight.

William Geake opened his eyes wide and answered curtly, "Yes: that's my wife—Naomi Geake. What then?"

The man scratched his head, contemplating William as he might some illegible sign-post set up at an unusually bothersome cross-road.

"She keeps very han'some, I will say." His smile grew still more ingratiating.

"Was you wishin' to speak wi' her?"

"Well, there! I was an' yet I wasn't. 'Tis terrible puzzlin'. You don't know me, I dessay."

"No, I don't."

"I be called Abe Bricknell—A-bra-ham Bricknell. I used to be Na'mi's husband, one time. There now"—with an accent of genuine contrition—"I felt sure 'twould put you out."

The tongue grew dry in William Geake's mouth, and the sunlight died off the road before him. He stared at a blister in the green paint of the garden-gate and began to peel it away slowly with his thumb-nail: then, pulling out his handkerchief, picked away at the paint that had lodged under the nail, very carefully, while he fought for speech.

"I be altered a brave bit," said Naomi's first husband, still with his silly smile.

"Come into th' house," William managed to say at last; and turning, led the way to the door. On his way he caught himself wondering why the hum of the bees had never sounded so loudly in the garden before: and this was all he could think about till he reached the doorstep. Then he turned.

"Th' Lord's ways be past findin' out," he said, passing a hand over his eyes.

"That's so: that's what *I* say mysel'," the other assented cheerfully, as if glad to find their wits jumping together.

"Man!" William rounded on him fiercely. "What's kept 'ee, all these years? Aw, man, man! do 'ee know what you've done?"

"I'd a sun-stroke," said the wanderer, tapping his head and still wearing his deprecatory smile; "a very bad sun-stroke. I sailed in the *John S. Hancock*. I dessay Na'mi told you about that, eh?"

"Get on wi' your tale."

"Pete Hancock was cap'n. The vessel was called after his uncle, you know, an' the Hancocks had a-bought up most o' the shares in her. That's how Pete came to be cap'n. We sailed on a Friday—unlucky, I've heard that is. But Pete said them that laid th' Atlantic cable had started that day an' broke the spell. Pete had a lot o' tales, but he made a poor cap'n; no head."

"Look here," put in "William with desperate calm," I don't want to know about Peter Hancock."

90

"There's not much to know if you did. He made a very poor cap'n, though it don't become one to say so, now he's gone. An affectionate man, though, for all his short-comin's. The last time he brought his vessel home from New Orleans he was in that pore to get back to his wife an' childer, he ripped along the Gulf Stream and pretty well ribbed the keelson out of her. Thought, I reckon, that since all the shareholders belonged to his family th' expense wouldn' be grudged. But I guess it made her tender. That's how she came to go down so suddent."

"She foundered?"

"I'm comin' to that. We'd just run our nose into the tropics an' was headin' down for Kingston Harbour—slippin' along at five knots easy an' steady, an' not a sign of trouble. The time, so far as I can tell, was somewhere near five bells in the middle watch. I'd turned in, leavin' Pete on deck, an' was fast asleep; when all of a suddent a great jolt sent me flyin' out o' the berth. As soon as I got my legs an' wits again I was up on deck, and already the barque was settlin' by the head like a burst crock. She'd crushed her breastbone in on a sunken tramp of a derelict—a dismasted water-logged lump, that maybe had been washin' about the Atlantic for twenty year' an' more before her app'inted time came to drift across our fair-way an' settle the hash o' the *John S. Hancock*. Sir, I reckon she went down inside o' five minutes. We'd but bare time to get out one boat and push clear o' the whirl of her. All hands jumped in; she was but a sixteen foot boat, an' we loaded her down to the gun'l a'most. There was a brave star-shine, but no moon. Cruel things happen 'pon the sea."

He passed a hand over his eyes, as if to brush off the film his sufferings had drawn across them. Then he pursued:

"Cruel things happen 'pon the sea. We'd no food nor drink but a tin o' preserved pears; Lord knows how that got there; but 'twas soon done. Pete had a small compass, a gimcrack affair hangin' to his watch-chain, an' we pulled by it west-sou'-west towards the nighest land, which we made out must be some one or another o' the Leeward Islands; but 'twas more to keep ourselves busy than for aught else: the boat was so low in the water that even with the Trade to help us, we made but a mile an hour, an' had to be balin' all day and all night. The third day, as the sun grew hot, two o' the men went mad. We had to pitch 'em overboard an' beat 'em off wi' the oars till they drowned: else they'd ha' sunk the boat. This seemed to hang on Pete's mind, in a way. All the next night he talked light-headed; said he could hear the dead men hailin' their names. About midnight he jumped after 'em—to fetch 'em, he said—an' was drowned. He took his compass with him, but that didn't make much odds. The boat was lighter now, an' we hadn' to bale. Pretty soon I got too weak to notice how the men went. I was lyin' wi' my head under the stern sheets an' only pulled mysel' up, now an' then, to peer out over the gun'l. I s'pose 'twas the splashes as the men went over that made me do this. I don't know for certain. There was sharks about: cruel things happen 'pon the sea. The boat was in a gashly cauch of blood too. One chap—Jeff Tresawna it was: his mother lived over to Looe—had tried to open a vein, to drink, an' had made a mess o't an' bled to death. Far as I know there was no fightin' to eat one another, same as one hears tell of now an' then. The men just went mad and jumped like sheep: 'twas a reg'lar disease. Two would go quick, one atop of t'other; an' then there'd be a long stillness, an' then a yellin' again an' two more splashes, maybe three. All through it I was dozin', off an' on; an' I reckon these things got mixed up an' repeated in my head: for our crew was only sixteen all told, an' it seemed to me I'd heard scores go over. Anyway I opened my eyes at last—night it was, an' all the stars blazin'—an' the boat was empty all except me an' Jeff Tresawna, him that had bled to death. He was lying up high in the bows, wi' his legs stretched Out towards me along the bottom-boards. There was a twinkle o' dew 'pon the thwarts an' gun'l, an' I managed to suck my shirt-sleeve, that was wringin' wet, an' dropped off dozin' again belike. The nex' thing I minded was a sort o' dream that I was home to Carne again, over Pendower beach—that's where my father an' mother lived. I heard the breakers quite plain. The sound of 'em woke me up. This was a little after daybreak. The sound kept on after I'd opened my eyes, though not so loud. I took another suck at my shirt-sleeve an' pulled myself up to my knees by the thwart an' looked over. 'Twas the sound o' broken water, sure enough, that I'd been hearing; an' 'twas breakin' round half a dozen small islands, to leeward, between me an' the horizon. I call 'em islands; but they was just rocks stickin' up from the sea, and birds on 'em in plenty; but otherwise, if you'll excuse the liberty, as bare as the top o' your head."

Geake nodded gravely, with set face.

"I've heard since," went on the seaman, "that these were bits, so to say, belongin' to the Leeward Islands, about eighty miles sou'west o' St. Kitt's. Our boat must ha' driven past St. Kitt's, but just out o' sight; or perhaps we'd passed a peep of it in the night-time. Well, as you'll be guessin' the boat was pretty nigh to one o' these islands, or I shouldn' ha' heard the wash. Half a mile off it was, I dessay, an' a pretty big wash. This was caused by the current, no doubt, for the wind was nex' to nothin', an' no swell around the boat. What's more, the current was takin' us, broadside on, pretty well straight for the rocks. There was no rudder an' only one oar left i' the boat; an' that was broke off short at the blade. But I managed to slip it over the starn an' made shift to keep her head straight. Her nose went bump on the shore, an' then she swung round an' went drivin' past: me not havin' strength left to put out a hand, much less to catch hold an' stop the way on us. We might ha' driven past an' off to sea again, if it hadn' been for a spit o' rock that reached out ahead. This brought us up short, an' there we lay an' bump'd for a bit. I dessay it took me half an hour to get out over the side: an' all the time I kept hold o' the broken oar. I dunno why I did this: but it saved my life afterwards. Hav'ee got such a thing as a drop o' cider in the house?"

"We go upon temperance principles here," said Geake. He rose and brought a jug of water and a glass.

"That'll do," said the wanderer, and helped himself. "Na'mi used to take a glass o' beer wi' her meals, I remember. Well, as I was agoin' to tell you, havin' got out o' the boat, I'd just sense enough left to clamber up above high-water mark, an' there I sat starin' stupid-like an' wonderin' how I'd done it. Down below, the boat was heavin' i' the wash an' joltin' 'pon the rocks, an' I watched her—bump, bump, up an' down, up an' down—wi' Jeff jamm'd by the shoulders i' the bows, and glazin' up at me wi' a silly blank face, like as if he couldn' make it all out. As the tide rose him up nearer, I crawled away further up. Seemed to me he an' the boat was after me like a sick dream, an' I grinned every time the timbers gave an extry loud crack. At last her bottom was stove, an' she filled very quiet an' went down. The wind was fresher by this an' some heavy clouds comin' up. Then it rained. I don't rightly know if this was the same day or no: can't fit in the days an' nights. But it rained heavy. There was a quill-feather lyin' close by my hand—the rock was strewed wi' feathers an' the birds' droppin's—an' with it I tried to get at the rain-water that was caught in the crannies o' the rocks. While I was searchin' about I came across an egg. It was stinkin', but I ate it. After that, feelin' a bit stronger, I'd a mind to fix up the oar for a mark, in case any vessel passed near an' me asleep or too weak to make a signal. I found a handy chink i' the rock to plant it in, an' a rovin' pain I had in my stomach while I was fixin' it. That was the egg, I dessay. An' my head in a maze, too: but I'd sense enough to think now what a fool I was not to have took Jeff's shirt off'n, to serve me for a flag. Hows'ever, my own bein' wringin' wet, an' the sun pretty strong just then, I slipped it off an' hitched it atop o' the oar to dry an' be a flag at the same time, till I could rig up some kind o' streamer, out o' the seaweed. An' then I was forced to vomit. And that's about the last thing, Mister Geake, I can mind doin'. 'Tis all foolishness after that. They tell me that a 'Merican schooner, the *Shawanee*, sighted my shirt flappin', an' sent a boat an' took me off an' landed me at New Orleens. My head was bad—oh, very bad—an' they put me in a 'sylum an' cured me. But they took eight year' over it, an' I doubt if 'tis much of a job after all. I wasn' bad all the time, I must tell you, sir; but 'tis only lately my mem'ry would work any further back 'n the wreck o' the barque. Everything seemed to begin an' end wi' that. 'Tis about a year back that some visitors came to the 'sylum. There was a lady in the party, an' something in her face, when she spoke to me, put me in mind o' Na'mi, an' I remembered I was a married man. Inside of a fortnight, part by thinkin'—'tis hard work still for me to think—part by dreamin', I'd a-worried it all out. I was betterin' fast by that. Soon as I was well enough to be discharged, I worked my passage home in a grain ship, the *Druid*, o' Liverpool. I was reckonin' all the way back that Na'mi'd be main glad to see me agen. But now I s'pose she won't."

"It'll come nigh to killin' her."

"I dessay, now, you two have got to be very fond? She used to be a partic'lar lovin' sort o' woman."

"I love her more 'n heaven!" William broke out; and then cowered as if he half expected to be struck with lightning for the words.

"I heard of her havin' married, down at the Fifteen Balls, at Troy. I dropped in there to pick up the news."

"What! You've been tellin' folks who you be!"

"Not a word. First of all I was minded to play off a little surprise 'pon old Toms, the landlord, who didn' know me from Adam. But hearin' this, just as I was a-leadin' up to my little joke, I thought maybe 'twould annoy Na'mi. She used to be very strict in some of her notions."

93

William Geake took two hasty turns up and down the little parlour. His Bible, in which before breakfast he had been searching for a text, lay open on the side table. Behind its place on the shelf was a small skivet he had let into the wall; and in that drawer was stored something over twenty-five pounds, the third of his savings. Geake kept a bank-account, and the balance lay at interest with Messrs. Climo and Hodges, of St. Austell. But he had the true countryman's aversion to putting all his eggs in one basket; and although Messrs. Climo and Hodges were safe as the Bank of England, preferred to keep this portion of his wealth in his own stocking. He closed the Bible hastily; rammed it back, upside down, in its place; then took it out again, and stood holding it in his two hands and trembling. He was living in sin: he was minded to sin yet deeper. And yet what had he done to deserve Naomi in comparison with the unspeakable tribulations this simple mariner had suffered? Sure, God must have preserved the fellow with especial care, and of wise purpose brought him through shipwreck, famine, and madness home to his lawful wife. The man had made Naomi a good husband. Had William Geake made her a better? (Husband?)— here he dropped the Bible down on the table again as if it burned his fingers. Whatever had to be done must be done quickly. Here was the innocent wrecker of so much happiness hanging on his lips for the next word, watching wistfully for his orders, like any spaniel dog. And Naomi would be back before nightfall. God was giving him no time: it was unfair to hustle a man in this way. In the whirl of his thoughts he seemed to hear Naomi's footfall drawing nearer and nearer home. He could almost upbraid the Almighty here for leaving him and Naomi childless. A child would have made the temptation irresistible.

"I wish a'most that I'd never called, if it puts you out so terrible," was the wanderer's plaintive remark after two minutes of silent waiting.

This sentence settled it. The temptation *was* irresistible. Geake unlocked the skivet, plunged a hand in and banged down a fistful of notes on the table.

"Here," said he; "here's five-an'-twenty pound'. You shall have it all if you'll go straight out o' this door an' back to America."

IV.

Half-an-hour later, William Geake was standing by his garden-gate again. Every now and then he glanced down the road towards St. Austell, and after each glance resumed his nervous picking at the blister of green paint that had troubled him earlier in the day. He was face to face with a new and smaller, but sufficiently vexing, difficulty. Abe Bricknell had gone, taking with him the five five-pound notes. So far so good, and cheap at the price. But the skivet was empty: and the day was Saturday: and every Saturday evening, as regularly as he wound up the big eight-day clock in the kitchen, Naomi and he would sit down and count over the money. True he had only to go to St. Austell and Messrs. Climo and Hodges would let him draw five new notes. The numbers would be different, and Naomi (prudent woman) always took note of the numbers: but some explanation might be invented. The problem was: How to get to St. Austell and back before Naomi's return? The distance was too great to be walked in the time; and besides, the coffin must be ready by nightfall. He had promised it; he was known for a man of his word; and owing to the morning's interruption it would be a tough job to finish, at the best. There was no help for it; and—so easy is the descent of Avernus—Geake's unaccustomed wits were already wandering in a wilderness of improbable falsehoods, when he heard the sound of wheels up the road, and Long Oliver came along in Farmer Lear's red-wheeled trap and behind Farmer Lear's dun-coloured mare. As he drew near at a trot he eyed Geake curiously, and for a moment seemed inclined to pull up, but thought better of it, and was passing with no more than a nod of the head and "good-day."

It was unusual, though, to see Long Oliver driving a horse and trap; and Geake, moreover, had a sudden notion.

"Good-mornin'," he answered; "whither bound?"

"St. Austell. I've a bit of business to do, so I'm takin' a holiday; in style, as you see."

"I wonder now," Geake suggested, forgetting all about the coffin, "if you'd give me a lift. I was just thinkin' this moment that I'd a bit o' business there that had clean slipped my mind this week."

This was transparently false to any one acquainted with Geake's methodical habits. Long Oliver screwed up his eyes.

"Can't, I'm afraid. I'm engaged to take up old Missus Oke an' her niece at Tippet's corner; an' the niece's box. The gal's goin' in to St. Austell, into service. So there's no room. But if there's any little message I can take—"

"When'll you be back?"

"Somewhere's about five I'll be passin'."

"Would 'ee mind waitin' a moment? I've a cheque I want cashed at Climo and Hodges for a biggish sum: but you'm a man I can trust to bring back the money safe."

"Sutt'nly," said Long Oliver.

Geake went into the house and wrote a short letter to the bankers. He asked them to send back by messenger, and in return for cheque enclosed, the sum of twenty-five pounds, in five new five-pound notes. He was aware (he said) that the balance of his running account was but a pound or two: but as they held something over fifty pounds of his on deposit, he felt sure they would oblige him and enable him to meet a sudden call.

"Twenty-five pounds is the sum," he explained; "an' you must be sure to get it in five-pound notes—*new five-pound notes*. You'll not forget that?" He closed the envelope and handed it up to Long Oliver, who buttoned it in his breast-pocket.

"You shall have it, Mr. Geake, by five o'clock this evenin'," said he, giving the reins a shake on the mare's back; "so 'long!" and he rattled off.

A mile, and a trifle more, beyond Geake's cottage, he came in sight of a man clad in blue sailor's cloth, trudging briskly ahead. Long Oliver's lips shaped themselves as if to whistle; but he made no sound until he overtook the pedestrian, when he pulled up, looked round in the man's face, and said—

"Abe Bricknell!"

The sailor came to a sudden halt, and went very white in the face.

"How do you know my name?" he asked, uneasily.

"'Recognised 'ee back in Troy, an' borrowed this here trap to drive after 'ee. Get up alongside. I've summat to say to 'ee."

Bricknell climbed up without a word, and they drove along together.

"Where was you goin'?" Long Oliver asked, after a bit.

"To Charlestown."

"To look for a ship?"

"Yes."

"Goin' back to America?"

"Yes."

"You've been callin' on William Geake: an' you didn' find Naomi at home."

"Geake don't want it known."

"That's likely enough. You've got twenty-five pound' o' his in your pocket."

Abe Bricknell involuntarily put up a hand to his breast.

"Ay, it's there," said Long Oliver, nodding. "It's odd now, but I've got twenty-five pound in gold in *my* pocket; an' I want you to swop."

"I don't take ye, Mister—"

"Long Oliver, I'm called in common. Maybe you remembers me?"

"Why, to be sure! I thought I minded your face. But still I don't take your meanin' azactly."

"I didn' suppose you would. So I'm goin' to tell 'ee. Fourteen year' back I courted Naomi, an' she used me worse 'n a dog. Twelve year' back she married you. Nine year' back you went to sea in the *John S. Hancock*, an' was wrecked off the Leeward Isles an' cast up on a spit o' rock. I'd been hangin' about New Orleens, just then, at a loose end, an' bein' in want o' cash, took a scamper in the *Shawanee*, a dirty tramp of a schooner knockin' in an' out and peddlin' notions among the West Indy Islanders. As you know we caught sight o' your signal an' took you off, an' you went to a mad-house. You was clean off your head an' didn' know me from Adam; an' I never let on that I knew you or the ship you'd sailed in. 'Seemed to me the hand o' God was in it, an' I saw my way to cry quits wi' Naomi."

"I don't see."

"I don't suppose you do. But 'twas this way:—Naomi (thinks I) 'll be givin' this man up afore long. She's a takeable woman, an' by-'n-bye, some new man'll set eyes on her. Then, thinks I, her banns'll be called in Church, an' I'll be there an' forbid 'em. Do 'ee see now?"

"That was very clever o' you," replied the simple seaman, and added with obvious sincerity, "I'm sure I should never ha' thought 'pon anything so clever as that. But why didn' you carry it out?"

"Because God Almighty was cleverer. Times an' times I'd pictured it up in my head how 'twould all work out; an' the parson in his surplice stuck all of a heap; an' the heads turnin' to look; an' the women faintin'. An' when the moment came for a man to claim her, what d'ye think she did? But there, a head like yours 'd never guess—*why she went to a Registry Office, an' there weren't no banns at all*. That overcame me. I seed the wisdom o' Providence from that hour. I be a converted man. An' I'm damned if I'll let you come along an' upset the apple-cart after all these years. Can 'ee write?"

"Tolerable, though I'm no hand at spellin'."

"Very well. We'll have a drink together at St. Austell, an' while we're there you shall do up Geake's notes in an envelope with a note sayin' your compliments, but on second thoughts you couldn't think o' takin' his money."

Bricknell's face fell somewhat.

"You gowk! You'll have twenty-five pound' o' mine in exchange: solid money, an' my own earnin's. I've more 'n that in my pocket here."

"But I don't see why *you* should want to give me money."

"An' you'm too mad to see if I explained. 'Tis a matter o' conscience, an' you may take it at that. When the letter's wrote—best not sign it, by the way, for fear of accidents—you give it to me an' I'll see Geake gets it to-night. After that's written I'll pay your fare to Liverpool, an' then you'll get a vessel easy. Now I see your mouth openin' and makin' ready to argue—"

"I was goin' to say, Long Oliver, that you seem to be actin' very noble, now: but 'twas a bit hard on *me*, your holdin' your tongue as you did."

"So 'twas, so 'twas. I reckon some folks is by nature easy forgotten, an' you'm one. If that's your character, I hope to gracious you'm goin' to keep it up. An' twenty-five pound' is a heap o' money for such a man as you."

"It is," the wanderer asserted. "Ay, I feel that."

At twenty minutes to five that evening, Long Oliver pulled up again by the green garden-gate. William Geake from his workshop had caught the sound of the mare's hoofs three minutes before, and awaited him.

"One, two, three, four, five." The notes were counted out deliberately. Long Oliver, having been thanked, gathered up his reins and suddenly set them down again.

"Dear me," said he, "if I hadn' almost forgot! I've a letter for 'ee, too."

"Eh?"

"Iss. A kind of a sailor-like lookin' chap came up to me i' the Half Moon yard as I was a takin' out the mare. 'Do you come from Gantick?' says he, seein' no doubt Farmer Lear's name 'pon the cart. 'There or thereabouts,' says I. 'Know Mister W. Geake?' says he. 'Well,' says I. 'Then, if you're passin', I wish you'd give 'en this here letter,' says he, an' that's all 'e said."

"I wonder who 'twas," said Geake. But his face was white.

"Don't know 'en by sight. Said 'e was in a great hurry for to catch the up train. Which puts me i' mind I must be movin' on. Good-night t'ye, neighbour!"

As soon as he had turned the corner, Geake opened the letter.

* * * * *

When Naomi returned, half-an-hour later, she found him standing at the gate as if he had spent the day there: as, indeed, he might have, for all the work done to the coffin.

"I must bide up to-night an' finish that job," he said, when they were indoors and she began asking how in the world he had been spending his time. "I've been worryin' mysel' all day."

"It's those sermons agen," Naomi decided. "They do your head no good, an' I wish you'd give up preachin'."

"Now that's just what I'm goin' to do," he answered, pushing the Bible far into the shelf till its edges knocked on the wood of the skivet-drawer.

THE PRINCE OF ABYSSINIA'S POST-BAG.

I.—AN INTERRUPTION:

From Algernon Dexter, writer of Vers de Societe, London, to Rasselas, Prince of Abyssinia.

My dear prince,—Our correspondence has dwindled of late. Indeed, I do not remember to have heard from you since I wrote to acknowledge your kindness in standing godfather to my boy Jack (now rising two), and the receipt of the beautiful scimitar which, as a christening present, accompanied your consent. Still I do not forget the promise you exacted from "Q." and myself after lunch at the Mitre, on the day when we took our bachelors' degrees together—that if in our paths through life we happened upon any circumstance that seemed to throw fresh light on the dark, complex workings of the human heart, or at least likely to prove of interest to a student of his fellow men, we would write it down and despatch it to you, under cover of The Negus. During the months of my engagement to Violet these communications of mine (you will allow) were frequent enough: since our marriage they have grown shamefully fewer. Possibly I lose alertness while I put on flesh: it is the natural hebetudus of happiness. "Q."—who is never seen now upon London stones—no doubt sends you a plenty of what passes for news in that parish which it is his humour to prefer to the Imperial City. But, believe me, the very finest romance is still to be had in London: and to prove this I am going to tell you a story that, upon my soul, Prince, will make you sit up.

Until last night the Seely-Hardwickes were a force in this capital. They were three,—Seely-Hardwicke himself, who owned a million or more, and to my knowledge drank Hollands and smoked threepenny Returns in his Louis Quinze library; Mrs. Seely-Hardwicke, as beautiful as the moon and clever to sinfulness; and Billy, their child, aged seven-and-a-half. To-day their whereabouts would be as difficult to find as that of the boy in Mrs. Hemans's ballad. You jump to the guess that they have lost their money. You are wrong.

It was amassed in the canned-fruit trade, which, I understand, does not fluctuate severely, though doubtless in the last instance dependent on the crops. Seely-Hardwicke and his wife were ready to lose any amount of it at cards, which accounts for a measure of their success. It had been found (with Mrs. Seely-Hardwicke) somewhere on the Pacific Slope, by a destitute Yorkshireman who had tired of driving rivets on the Clyde and betaken himself across the

Atlantic, for a change, in front of a furnace some thirty-odd feet below decks. Of his adventures in the Great Republic nothing is known but this, that he drove into the silence of its central plain at the tail of a traction engine and emerged on its western shore, three years later, with a wife, a child and a growing pile. With this pile there grew a desire to spend it in his own country; and the family landed at Liverpool on Billy's sixth birthday. I think their double-barrelled name must have been invented by Mrs. Seely-Hardwicke on the voyage.

I first made Billy's acquaintance in the Row, where a capable groom was teaching him to ride a very small skewbald pony. This happened in the week after our Jack was born, when I was perforce companionless: but as soon as Violet could ride again, she too fell a victim to the red curls and seraphic face of this urchin. And so, when Billy's mother began, later in the season, to appear in the Row, Billy (now promoted to a larger pony) introduced us in his own fashion and we quickly made friends. By this time she had been "presented," and was fairly on her feet in London: and henceforward her career resembled not so much a conquest as the progress of a Roman Emperor. I am not referring to the vulgar achievements of mere wealth. Wherever these people went, to be sure, they left outposts—a Mediterranean villa, a deer forest behind the Grampians, small Saturday-to-Monday establishments beside the Thames and the North Sea, and furnished abodes on short leases near Newmarket and Ascot Heaths; not to mention nomadic trifles such as houseboats and yachts. Any one with money can purchase these, and any one having a cook can fill them with people of a sort. The quality of Mrs. Seely-Hardwicke's success was seen in this, that from the first she knew none but the right people: and though, as her circle widened, it included names of higher and yet higher lustre, yet (if I may press a somewhat confused metaphor) its rings were concentric and hardly distinct. She never, I believe, was forced to drop an old acquaintance because she had found a new one. The just estimate of our Western manners which you, my dear Prince, formed at Balliol, will enable you to grasp the singularity of such a triumph. Its rapidity, I must admit, perplexes me still. But in those old days we studied Arnold Toynbee overmuch and neglected the civilising influences of the card-table. By the time the Seely-Hardwickes took their house near Hyde Park Corner, philanthropy was beginning to stale and our leaders to perceive that the rejuvenation of society must be effected (if at all) not by bestowing money on the poor, but by losing it to the rich. Seely-Hardwicke himself was understood to spend most of his time in the City, looking after the interests of canned fruits and making small fortunes out of his redundant cash.

You will readily understand that we soon came to see little of our new acquaintances. A small private income and the trivial wage commanded by society verses in this country (so different in many respects from Abyssinia) confined us to a much narrower orbit. But we were invited pretty often to their dinners, and the notes I have given you were taken on these occasions. Last night there were potentates at Mrs. Seely-Hardwicke's—several imported, and one of British growth. To-day—but you shall hear it in the fewest words.

Three days back, Billy failed to turn up in the Row. We met his mother riding alone and asked the reason. She told us the child had a cough and something of a sore throat and she thought it wiser to keep him at home.

On the next day, and yesterday, he was still absent. In the evening we went to the Seely-Hardwicke's dance. The thing was wonderfully done. An exuberant vegetation that suggested a virgin forest was qualified by the presence of several hundred people. It was impossible to dance or to feel lonely; and our hostess looked radiant as the moon in the reflected rays of her success. We shook hands with her and were swallowed in the crowd.

About half-an-hour later, as I watched the crush from a recess beside an open window and listened to the waltz that the band was playing, Seely-Hardwicke himself thrust his way towards me. He was crumpled and perspiring copiously: but the glory of it all sat on his blunt face yet more openly than on his wife's lovely features.

"I've not been here above ten minutes," he explained. "Had to run down to Liverpool suddenly last night, and only reached King's Cross something less 'n an hour back. Quick work."

"How's Billy?" I asked, after a few commonplace words.

"Off colour, still. I went up to see him, just now: but the nurse wouldn't let him be disturbed; said he was sleepin'. Best thing for him. You'll see him out, as lively as a lark, to-morrow."

"And getting stopped, as usual, by the police for expounding his idea of a canter in the Ladies' Mile."

He laughed. "Hey? I like that. I like spirit. He looks fragile—he's like his mother for that—but they're game every inch, the pair of 'em. You may think me silly, but I don't know that I can last out this without runnin' up to have a look at him. I haven't seen him for two days."

I believe he was on the point of launching out into any number of fatherly confidences. But at this point he was claimed by an acquaintance some ten paces off; and, plunging among his guests, was lost to me.

I cannot tell you, my dear Prince, how much time elapsed between this and the arrival of the home-grown Potentate—as you must allow me to call him until we meet and I can whisper his august name. But I know that shortly after his arrival, while I still loafed in my recess and hoped that Violet would soon drift in my direction and allow herself to be taken home, the throng around me began to thin in a most curious manner. How it happened—whence it started and how it spread—I cannot tell you. Only it seemed as if something began to be whispered, and the whisper melted the crowd like sugar. Almost before I grew aware of what was happening, I could see the far side of the room, and the Potentate there by Mrs. Seely-Hardwicke's side; and could mark their faces. His was cast in a polite, but slightly rigid smile. His eyes wandered. That supernumerary sense which all his family possesses had warned him that something was wrong. Mrs. Seely-Hardwicke's face was white as chalk, though her eyes returned his smile.

At this moment Violet came towards me.

"Take me home," she commanded, but under her breath. As she said it she shivered.

"What on earth is the matter?" I demanded.

She pulled me by the sleeve. I looked up and saw a white-haired man, of military carriage, walking towards His Royal Highness. He came to a halt, a pace off, and stood as if anxious to speak. I saw also that Mrs. Seely-Hardwicke would not allow him a chance, but talked desperately. I saw groups of people, up and down the room, regarding her even as we. And then the door was flung open.

Seely-Hardwicke came running in with Billy in his arms—or rather, with Billy's body. The child had died at four that afternoon, of diphtheria.

I got Violet out of the room as soon as I could. The man's language was frightful—filthy. And his wife straightened herself up and answered him back. It was a babel of obscene Frisco curses: but I remember one clear sentence of hers from the din—

"You—, you! And d'ye think *my* heart won't go to pieces when my stays are cut?"

* * * * *

All the way home Violet kept sobbing and crying out that she was never driven so slowly. She was convinced that some harm had happened to her own Jack. She ran up to the night-nursery at once and woke your god-child out of a healthy sleep. And he arose in his full strength and yelled.

II.—THE GREAT FIRE ON FREETHY'S QUAY.

From "Q."

Troy Town.

New Year's Eve, 1892.

MY DEAR PRINCE,—The New Year is upon us, a season which the devout Briton sets aside for taking stock of his short-comings. I know not if Prester John introduced this custom among the Abyssinians: but we find it very convenient here.

In particular I have been vexing myself to-day over the gradual desuetude of our correspondence. Doubtless the fault is mine: and doubtless I compare very poorly with Dexter, whose letters are bound to be bright and frequent. But Dexter clings to London; and from London, as from your own Africa, *semper aliquid novi.* But of Troy during these twelve months there has been little or nothing to delate. The small port has been enjoying a period of quiet which even the General Election, last summer, did not seriously disturb. As you know, the election turned on the size of mesh proper to be used in the drift-net fishery. We wore favours of red, white and blue, symbolising our hatred of the mesh favoured by Mr. Gladstone; and carried our man. Had other constituencies as sternly declined to fritter away their voting strength upon side issues, Lord Salisbury would now be in power with a solid majority at his back.

My purpose, however, is not to talk of politics, but to give you a short description of an event which has greatly excited us, and redeemed from monotony (though at the eleventh hour) the year Eighteen ninety-two. I refer to the great fire on Freethy's Quay, where Mr. Wm. Freethy has of late been improving his timber-store with a number of the newest mechanical inventions; among others, with a steam engine which operates on a circular saw, and impels it to cut up oak poles (our winter fuel) with incredible rapidity. It was here that the outbreak occurred, on Christmas Eve—of all days in the year—between five and six o'clock in the afternoon.

But I should first tell you that our town has enjoyed a long immunity from fires; and although we possess a Volunteer Fire Brigade, at once efficient and obliging, and commanded by Mr. Patrick Sullivan (an Irishman), the men have had little or no opportunity of combating their sworn foe. The Brigade was founded in the early autumn of 1873, and presented by public subscription with a handsome manual engine and a wooden house to contain it. This house, painted a bright vermilion, is a conspicuous object at the top of the hill above the town, as you turn off towards the Rope-walk. The firemen, of course, wear an appropriate uniform, with brazen helmets and shoulder-straps and a neat axe apiece, suspended in a leathern case from the waistband. But the spirit of make-believe has of necessity animated all their public exercise, if I except the 13th of April, 1879, when a fire broke out in the back premises of Mr. Tippett, carpenter. His shop was (and is) situated in the middle of the town, and in those days a narrow gatehouse gave, or rather prevented, access to the town on either side. These houses stood, one at the extremity of North Street, beside the Ferry Slip, the other at the south end of the Fore Street, where it turns the corner by the Ship Inn and mounts Lostwithiel Hill. With their low-browed arches, each surmounted by a little chamber for the toll-keeper, they recalled in an interesting manner the days when local traffic was carried on solely by means of pack-horses; but by an unfortunate oversight their straitness had been left out of account by the donors of the fire-engine, which stuck firmly in the passage below Lostwithiel Hill and could be drawn neither forwards nor back, thus robbing the Brigade of the result of six years' practice. For the engine filled up so much of the thoroughfare that the men could neither climb over nor round it, but were forced to enter the town by a circuitous route and find, to their chagrin, Mr. Tippett's premises completely gutted. For three days all our traffic entered and left the town perforce by the north side; but two years after, on the completion of the railway line to Troy, these obstructive gatehouses were removed, to give passage to the new Omnibus.

Let me proceed to the story of our more recent alarm. At twenty minutes to five, precisely, on Christmas Eve, Mr. Wm. Freethy left his engine-room by the door which opens on the Quay; turned the key, which he immediately pocketed; and proceeded towards his mother's house, at the western end of the town, where he invariably takes tea. The wind was blowing strongly from the east, where it had been fixed for three days, and the thermometer stood at six degrees below freezing. Indeed, I had remarked, early in the morning, that an icicle of quite respectable length (for a small provincial town), depended from the public water-tap under the Methodist Chapel. About twenty minutes after Mr. Freethy's departure, some children, who were playing about the Quay, observed dense volumes of smoke (as they thought) issuing from under the engine-room door. They gave the alarm. I happened to be in the street at the time, purchasing muscatels for the Christmas snap-dragon, and, after rushing up to the Quay to satisfy myself, proceeded with all haste to Mr. Sullivan, Captain of the Brigade.

I found him at tea, but behaving in a somewhat extraordinary manner. It is well known that Mr. and Mrs. Sullivan suffer occasionally from domestic disagreement, due, in great measure, to the lady's temper. Mr. Sullivan was sitting at the table with a saucer inverted upon his head, a quantity of tea-leaves matted in his iron-grey hair, and their juice trickling down his face. On hearing my alarming intelligence, he said:

"I had meant to sit there for some time; indeed, until my little boy returns with the Vicar, whom I have sent for to witness the effects of my wife's temper. I was sitting down to tea when I heard a voice in the street calling 'Whiting!'—a fish of which I am extremely fond—and ran out to procure threepenny worth. On my return, my wife here—I suppose, because she objects to clean the fish— assaulted me in the manner you behold."

With praiseworthy public spirit, however, Mr. Sullivan forewent his revenge, and, having cleansed his hair, ran with all speed to get out the fire-engine.

Returning to the Quay, at about 5 p.m., I found a large crowd assembled before the engine-room door, from which the vapour was pouring in dense clouds. The Brigade came rattling up with their manual in less than ten minutes. As luck would have it, this was just the hour when the mummers, guise dancers and darkey-parties were dressing up for their Christmas rounds; and the appearance presented by the crowd in the deepening dusk would, in less serious circumstances, have been extremely diverting. Two of the firemen wore large moustaches of burnt cork beneath their helmets, and another (who was cast to play the Turkish Knight) had found no time to remove the bright blue dye he had been applying to his face. The pumpmaker had come as Father Christmas, and the blacksmith (who was forcing the door) looked oddly in an immense white hat, a flapping collar and a suit of pink chintz with white bone buttons. He had not accomplished his purpose when I heard a shout, and, looking up the street, saw Mr. Wm. Freethy approaching at a brisk run. He is forty-three years old, and his figure inclines to rotundity. The wind, still in the east, combined with the velocity of his approach to hold his coat-tails in a line steadily horizontal. In his right hand he carried a large slice of his mother's home-made bread, spread with yellow plum jam; a semicircular excision of the crumb made it plain that he had been disturbed in his first mouthful. The crowd parted and he advanced to the door; laid his slice of bread and jam upon the threshold; searched in his fob pocket for the key; produced it; turned it in the lock; picked up his bread and jam again; opened the door; took a bite; and plunged into the choking clouds that immediately enveloped his person.

While the concourse waited, in absolute silence, the atmosphere of the engine-house cleared as if by magic, and Mr. Wm. Freethy was visible again in the converging rays of six bull's-eye lanterns held forward by six members of the Fire Brigade. One hand still held the bread and jam; the other grasped a stop-cock which he had that instant turned, shutting off the outpour of steam we had taken for smoke. Some one tittered; but the general laugh was prevented by a resounding splash. The recoiling crowd had backed against the fire-engine outside, and inadvertently thrust it over the Quay's edge into two fathoms of water!

We left it there till the tide should turn, and forming into procession, marched back through the streets. I never witnessed greater enthusiasm. I do not believe Troy held a man, woman, or child that did not turn out of doors to cheer and laugh. Presently a verse sprang up:—

"The smoke came out at Freethy's door,
An' down came Sullivan with his corps.
'My dears,' says Freethy,' don't 'ee pour!
For the smoke be steam an' nothin' more—
But what hav' 'ee done wi' the En-gine?'"

And the firemen, by shouting it as heartily as the rest, robbed the epigram of all its sting.

But the best of it, my dear Prince, was still to come. For at half-past eight (that being the time of low water) a salvage corps assembled and managed to drag the engine ashore by means of stout tackle hitched round the granite pedestal that stands on Freethy's Quay to commemorate the visit of Queen Victoria and Prince Albert, who landed there on the 8th of September, 1846. The guise-dancers paraded it through the streets until midnight, when they gave it over to the carollers, who fed it with buckets; and as the poor machine was but little damaged, brisk jets of water were made to salute the citizens' windows simultaneously with the season's holy songs. I, who have a habit of sleeping with my window open, received an icy shower-bath with the opening verse of "Christians, awake! Salute the Happy Morn...."

On Saturday next the Brigade assembles for a Grand Salvage Banquet in the Town Hall. There will be speeches. Accept, my dear Prince, all possible good wishes for the New Year....

"Q."

CPSIA information can be obtained at www.ICGtesting.com
Printed in the USA
BVOW04s1530210914

367738BV00019B/261/P

9 781500 340230